I0545333

ESCAPADES
Trident Ink Book 1

Lilly Atlas

All rights reserved. This book or any portion thereof may not be reproduced or used in any manner whatsoever without the express written permission of the author except for the use of brief quotations in a book review.

Copyright © 2018 Lilly Atlas

All rights reserved.

Lilly Atlas Books LLC

ISBN-13: 978-1-946068-22-4
ISBN-10: 1-946068-22-5

For Sam.
Thank you from the bottom of my heart for all your love, support, and assistance. But mostly for your spreadsheets.

Table of Contents

ESCAPADES
Trident Ink Book 1

CHAPTER ONE

Beautiful didn't come close to capturing the woman waiting for him at a cozy two-person table in the most romantic restaurant in town.

Stunning. Alluring. Captivating. Breathtaking. Sexy as fuck. And the adjectives just grew more X-rated from there.

Really, she was just gorgeous, plain and simple, with her hypnotic blue eyes and golden blond hair flowing down her back in stylish waves. Damn, he was a sucker for blondes. Always had been. And the longer the hair, the better.

There wasn't much that topped wrapping long silky strands of feminine hair around his fist and tipping his woman's head back, exposing her delicate neck as he plunged in and out of her tight body. Perfect opportunity to feast on the exposed skin of her throat. She would moan and arch into him—

Shit.

Derek's cock began to fill despite the fact he was standing outside a restaurant in the chilly November evening.

Well, really, what did it matter if he was aroused beyond reason?

This entire date was a prelude to sex. First order of business was to walk in and make nice. Flash charming smiles. Be charismatic and witty during the meal. Then leave together and find a secluded place to fuck each other's brains out.

So, what did it matter if he was hard now? His date knew the drill. Hell, this entire charade was her idea to begin with.

He blew out a harsh breath, fogging the restaurant's front window with the warmth of his exhalation. Time to go in. He'd stalled long enough. For some reason, a brick of nervousness had settled in his stomach the moment he spotted the expensive Georgetown restaurant.

The promise of sex wasn't what made him nervous. In fact, the opposite was true. Sex was something he was pretty damned certain he excelled at. Excelled at and loved.

So, why the unease? Christ, he'd faced down terrorists for years as a SEAL. He'd spent years in life-threatening situations without so much as blinking. And now he was afraid?

Perhaps it had something to do with the fact that for the past two years—shit, he still couldn't wrap his mind around that insane span of time—the only thing to come into contact with his dick was the palm and five fingers of his right hand. And maybe the left a time or two.

To think of all he'd taken for granted. The months he'd lost due to…what? How he'd allowed this to happen was still a giant mystery. One he needed to spend some serious time and brain power solving. It was the only way to fix it. To ensure it never happened again. No matter what life threw at him. No matter how deep the pain cut, how suffocating the grief became, he could not neglect this part of his life again. Could not neglect her again.

Next to him, a loud throat cleared, causing him to flinch. "Excuse me, sir?" The maître d' stood just three feet away, bouncing on the balls of his feet, no doubt to keep warm blood pulsing through his veins.

"Yes?"

"That lovely young woman in there you seem to be staring at through the window claims you may be here to join her." A cloud of steam drifted from his mouth as he spoke. His smile was questioning, like he was dying to ask why the hell Derek was standing outside freezing his ass off while a smoking hot woman waited for him inside.

How long had he been staring at the breath-fogged pane without actually seeing anything? He wiped a gloved hand through the cloudy condensation. Sure enough, clear blue eyes with a hint of mischief met his. She offered a half smile as one light eyebrow rose in question as if to ask, "You coming any time soon?"

Sooner than she knew if she kept looking at him like she was starving, and he was the only thing that could satisfy her hunger. It had been a long time since she'd looked at him like that.

"Yes. I'm here for her." The words were gruffer than he'd meant them to be but the idea of another man, any man, admiring his date was unacceptable. He'd always been a bit of a possessive beast. Not in a controlling and creepy way, but he sure as hell didn't share.

"Excellent, sir." The maître d' held the door and permitted Derek to pass into the restaurant. "Allow me to escort you to your table."

"Thank you," Derek said, his gaze riveted on his date. He was so captivated by her he nearly missed the ambiance of the restaurant. Low lighting and flickering candles gave the upscale steakhouse a romantic vibe. The place wasn't exactly his style. He'd always been more of a beer and wings kind of guy, but he could play the part of a classy gentleman for a few hours. Especially if the gig bought him a non-self-induced orgasm.

Garlic, peppered beef, and the aroma of expensive wine blended together, making his mouth water for more than just a taste of the woman waiting for him.

"Here we are, sir." The maître d' pulled out a sturdy wooden chair with one hand and extended a menu with the other.

"Thank you," Derek said. It was as much a dismissal as an expression of gratitude. He wanted, needed, a few minutes alone with his date before being interrupted by restaurant staff.

"Hi," she said. Her eyes glowed with genuine pleasure and a radiant smile spread across her face. He missed that smile. Missed it like he'd miss oxygen. "Glad you finally decided to join me."

"Hello, Kristin," he said, not missing the twitch of her lips when he said the name.

"Jake," she replied with a sassy smile.

He answered her mirth with a chuckle of his own. But he'd agreed to play the game from the get-go. No real names. Pure fantasy for one night. A chance for them to lose themselves in a sexual escapade devoid of past pain, baggage, and heartache.

"Not joining you was never an option, gorgeous. I just saw you through the window and couldn't tear myself away from the view."

"You're sweet." She flushed as though unaccustomed to compliments. Damn shame. A woman like her deserved to hear it daily. The man in her life must be such a fool—guilt churned in his stomach at the thought that he was that fool.

He shook it off. "What are you drinking?"

She lifted the wineglass to her glossy coral lips and took a delicate sip. "It's a Spanish Rioja. Delicious." A tiny purple drop remained on her plump lower lip.

Derek couldn't help it. As though on autopilot, he reached across the small table and captured the bead with his thumb. With his eyes on hers, he brought his finger to his mouth and licked. "You're right. Delicious."

Her throat worked as she swallowed, and a pink flush that had nothing to do with the warmth radiating from a nearby fireplace coated her skin. It was desire, hot, passionate, and more intoxicating than the wine.

There was no way in hell his body wasn't going to respond in kind. Blood rushed to his cock so fast the immediate stiffening was almost painful.

The air between them and surrounding their table popped and crackled with electricity. If it was up to him, they'd skip the meal entirely and find a quiet place where he could peel her out of that slinky black dress hugging her body in the most sinful way. But, this was her show, so he'd stick it out through the first act, but not much more than that.

"So," he said, settling into his seat, resigned to the fact that the meal would be spent with an iron rod between his legs. "Tell me about your week." As he spoke, he rolled the sleeves of his royal blue dress shirt to just below his elbows. Their proximity to the fireplace had him a bit overheated.

Or maybe it was just the proximity to his date.

Her gaze was fixed on his forearms and her eyes flared as each colorful inch of inked skin was revealed. "Well," she said her voice husky, "I've been out of work for a while due to…difficult circumstances and I just recently went back."

The breath seized in his lungs and he stalled his movement. How did he not know she'd just gone back to work? Was his head really that far up his own ass?

Difficult circumstances.

He almost snorted out loud. That was quite a benign way to describe what she'd been through over the past couple years. What they'd both been through. But tonight wasn't about wallowing in the agony of the past. It was about forging forward, connecting, pleasing one another.

"How did it go? Your first day?" His voice was hardly above a whisper. Deep emotions pummeled him from all directions as he looked straight into her slightly sad eyes. Emotions seeking to destroy the thick wall he'd erected over the past two years. Emotions he hadn't allowed himself to feel and still didn't want to deal with because they were guaranteed to bring an off-the-charts level of pain.

Her entire face lit up. "It was wonderful. Scary, exciting, fulfilling…really, really good."

Her enthusiasm was contagious, and Derek found himself shedding the dark mood from seconds before. Later that night, when he was alone, he'd allow himself to finally feel. To face the demons chasing him. For the moment, and for the rest of his date, he'd focus solely on the amazing woman dining with him.

She was what was important. Too bad it had taken him so long to remember that.

CHAPTER TWO

"So...*Jake*, what looks good to you?" Kristin asked as she opened her menu.

"You look pretty damn good." It was hard not to laugh at her playful use of the evening's pseudonym. He wanted to hear his real name fall off her lips, particularly later when she was crying out in ecstasy from the orgasms he'd give her. But the more he contemplated, he realized the plan had been smart all along.

The sense of anonymity that accompanied the use of an alias was freeing. It allowed him to fully sink into the role of a man without a history. He could pretend the past few years never existed, if only for a few hours, and that's exactly what was necessary to pull himself out of the sucking vortex of quicksand his life had a become.

She laughed, the sound full-bodied and vibrant, doing nothing to kill his arousal. "I meant from the menu. Not that you don't look edible yourself. I like that color blue on you. Her smile was radiant. The smile of a woman who was truly content in the moment.

He'd worn black slacks and a gray tie with his royal blue button up shirt. It took a lot to get him out of his uniform of T-shirts and jeans and into anything resembling formal wear. But he'd do damn near anything for more of those smiles.

Conversation flowed easily after that. Derek ordered a medium rare NY strip steak and a potato with all the fixings while Kristin requested a petite filet with a side of steamed spinach. They laughed, flirted, and drank another glass of wine before polishing off the meal. Once the plates had been cleared, there wasn't anything holding them back from what they both really wanted from the evening.

Her hot gaze connected with his. She was a small woman, though not a twig, and it was obvious two generous glasses of wine had relaxed her. She didn't appear drunk, just...happy, with relaxed shoulders, a constant smile, and twinkling eyes.

"Well, that was delicious. Thank you, Jake," she said as the waiter returned his credit card and receipt.

"My pleasure." Not yet, but it damn sure would be soon enough. Both of their pleasures, actually. Hers a few more times than his if all went according to plan.

"How'd you get here?" she asked, rimming the lip of her empty wineglass with a fingertip.

He kept his eyes glued to the motion, imagining that one finger trailing across his naked skin in a fiery path. "What? Oh, I drove." The ability to concentrate was flying out the window. If they didn't leave soon he just might lunge across the table and ravish her on the restaurant floor.

"Do you have a large car?" Her smile grew impish.

What was she up to? She knew damn well he drove an Escalade. "I do."

She rose from the table and he got his first view of her entire outfit. The black dress was simple, yet clung to her curves and highlighted everything he liked best about this woman's body. The deep V-neck showed off a moderate amount of cleavage, just enough to have him imagining how her breasts would quiver when he ran his tongue across the top of the mounds. The hemline stopped shy of midway down her thighs and damn if his hands didn't twitch with the desire to smooth their way up the silky skin that disappeared under the tight skirt.

With slow, sultry steps, she came around to his side of the table and leaned down until she was level with his ear. "Then maybe we should test out just how roomy the back seat is."

As she returned to her full height of only five-foot-four plus a few bonus inches due to heels, Derek gave in to the overwhelming temptation and slid his large hand around the back of her knee. His fingers weren't soft, but despite the calluses, he felt just how velvety her skin was. He coasted his hand up the back of her thigh until it disappeared under her skirt. But he didn't stop there. Higher and higher he went. Indecently high, maintaining eye contact the entire time.

His thumb brushed the underside of her rounded ass as his fingers encountered a tiny swatch of fabric covering her opening. Her very hot, very wet opening.

"Jesus," he whispered at the same time she let out a small gasp.

"Please, Jake." A light shade of pink stole across her face. A mixture of desire and bashfulness due to the public display. A contradiction that drew him to her right off the bat. Intense sensuality combined with a private, almost shy nature.

"What is it you want, Al—um, Kristin?" Shit. He'd stumbled over her fake name. Would she notice? Would it bring reality back to the encounter and end the game?

"I want you to fuck me." Her voice was low in deference to other customers. He almost laughed out loud. Like it mattered at this point. Sure, their table was in the back corner of the restaurant, but she was standing with his hand buried under her dress, coating his fingers with her arousal. Modesty had died a quick death.

He was so hard, he wasn't entirely certain he'd be able to get up and walk out of the restaurant without hobbling. A knowing glint shone in her eyes, as though she was well aware of his predicament and found it amusing. "Well?" she asked, teasing in her voice.

Two could play this game. He withdrew his hand from its warm prison between her thighs, brought a finger to his mouth, and licked the tip. Her eyes flared, and her breath hitched. "Damnit, D—Jake. No more playing. Please take me out of here. I need your hands on me, all over me."

That was about all of the teasing Derek could handle as well. He stood, shoving his chair back so hard it teetered on its hind legs, and grabbed Kristin's hand. Halfway to the exit, his brain cleared enough to realize he was all but dragging her through the restaurant. "Sorry," he mumbled as he slowed and gave her hand a gentle squeeze.

"It's fine. I'm in just as much of a hurry as you are," she said from behind him.

The maître d' held the door for them and shot Kristin a wink as they left the restaurant. If Derek wasn't in such a frenzy to get her naked, he'd have stopped and let the man know just how much he appreciated another man flirting with her.

She barely seemed to notice though, keeping pace with him as they hurried into the parking garage one block down from the restaurant. The dark garage was quiet except for the rapid click-clack of her heels on the concrete. He kept his hand low on the bare skin of her back as he guided her toward the vehicle. That damn dress dipped in the back, exposing creamy skin, and he honestly couldn't say whether he preferred the view from the front or the back. There was something about the smooth curves of a woman's naked back that was sexy as fuck.

When they reached his black Escalade, he held the door open and she climbed into the back seat, giving him an up close and personal view of her stellar ass as she crawled across the seat. Thank God, the windows were tinted. He wasn't sure he could have driven them anywhere in his state. As long as she didn't scream the place down, none of the unsuspecting individuals searching for their cars would have a clue what was going on inside the vehicle.

As he slid into the back seat after the woman who was about to rock his world, his hands shook. Shit. He was nervous as hell. Not once in his life had he been nervous to be with a woman. Not even when he'd lost his virginity at fifteen to his homecoming date in her parents' basement.

But now? Now he was trembling worse than a virgin bride on her wedding night.

Get it together, asshole.

Somehow, he managed to flick the dome light on without betraying how unsteady he was.

The moment he glanced at the woman waiting for him to make a move, all his doubts were replaced by intense desire. She'd kicked off the heels and rested with her back propped against the rear passenger door, both legs bent at the knee and braced on the leather seat giving him a view straight up her dress. The darkened swatch of fabric covering her pussy called to him like a siren's song.

Forgetting all thoughts of guilt, neglect, or regrets, he closed the distance between them and knelt between her thighs.

"Give me your mouth."

She obeyed his order without hesitation. No games and no more teasing. Just upturned lips and the rapid rise and fall of her chest as her anticipation grew. He captured her lips in a kiss full of two years of pent-up hunger.

The flavor of wine lingered on her tongue, adding to her natural sweetness. He took command of the kiss, sliding a hand around the back of her neck and holding her just where he wanted her. She gave as good as she got, nipping at his lips and moaning into his mouth as she arched into him.

He groaned as she rubbed against him, her hot core burning into his leg. As he continued to kiss her like he'd die without it, he nudged his thick thigh tighter into the notch between her legs. She whimpered and ground herself against him.

After a few moments of making out and dry humping like teenagers, she began trembling and Derek smiled against her mouth. It wouldn't be long before she lost control. He deepened the kiss, in full command of her body at that moment. Just how he liked it. He never put any labels on himself or the way he liked to fuck, but one thing was for sure, he craved being in control at all times.

Her shivers increased, and he eased his thigh back. She would come multiple times tonight, but the first would be around his cock. Squeezing him and holding him in her body while she lost herself.

"No, J-Jake, more." She moaned and lifted herself against him, but he'd moved too far out of her reach.

With a chuckle, he ended the kiss and stared down at her. She panted beneath him, her eyes glazed and shining with lust. At the tips of her heaving breasts, her nipples beaded against the fabric of the snug dress.

"Christ, you're so fucking beautiful." His language tended to deteriorate when his brain was flooded with high levels of testosterone. Not that it was very proper to begin with.

"Thank you," she whispered.

Guilt and regret scratched at the back of his neck, trying to worm their way into the car and between them. Try as he might, the feelings were too strong to ignore. How could he have— He shook his head. He'd been so stupid, taken so many things for granted.

"Hey." She cupped his cheek in her small hand. "I sure hope you aren't done with me yet. Because I got to tell you, I've played out this date in my head a hundred times over the past few days and none of those times did it end with a quick make-out session in the back of your car."

"Oh yeah?" he asked. "How did it end?" Some of the invading gloom dissipated.

"Usually with you telling me what a sex goddess I am and how you've never come so hard in your life." She winked.

This time his laugh was loud and genuine. She was exactly what he'd needed. The only thing he'd ever needed. He shoved away the last of the negative thoughts. They had no place between them. Not in that moment.

For him, the time was fast approaching. Time to let the thoughts in and deal with them even though he wanted to continue running from them. But where had running gotten him? It brought nothing but loneliness and lack of physical affection. Damn, he was a fool.

"What about me? Will you tell me I'm a sex god?"

A saucy grin lit her face. "Guess that remains to be seen."

CHAPTER THREE

Finally.

What he'd been denied—denying himself—for so long was right there in front of him. Soft, warm, vibrant. Making him laugh and remember that there was more to life than wallowing in self-pity. All he had to do was reach out and take it.

And he damn well planned to. Again, and again.

"Scoot down," he said.

He shifted his weight back, and she shimmied down until she was lying flat on the bench seat of the Escalade's back row.

"I need to see more of you." Needed to gaze upon the body he'd only been privy to in his dreams and fantasies for two years. With unsteady hands, he tried to draw the straps of the dress down her shoulders, but he couldn't maneuver it properly in the tight space of the car.

"Fuck it," he said, making her giggle. A growl rose in his throat as he pulled the V of her dress wide, exposing her bare breasts. As in no bra. Just stiff nipples on display to his hungry gaze. Shit if he'd know that, he might have skipped the meal altogether. "Jesus, you're so fucking sexy." There was no finesse to the way he manhandled the fabric to keep it out of the way.

As soon as she was exposed to him, he latched on to a nipple and sucked it deep into his mouth. She cried out and fisted his short hair in her hands, holding his head against her as though there was a chance in hell he'd stop what he was doing. With his tongue, he rhythmically pressed the taut bud to the roof of his mouth.

"Oh, D-Jake. That feels so good. It's been so long. More, more."

It was the understatement of the year, but he agreed with how fucking good it was. The taste of her flooded his system like a drug. He moved to the other breast, this time seizing her nipple between his teeth and giving a less than gentle nip.

She went wild beneath him, bucking and pulling his hair while nonsensical words flowed from her. "Jake! Inside me, now. I can't wait. Now, now, now."

God, he loved her like this. Wild, begging for him, desperate to feel him. "I'll make it up to you," he said as he fumbled with his belt and zipper.

"What?" Her lust-filled eyes grew confused. "Make what up to me?"

"I'm so fuckin' close to the edge, this first time might only last five seconds. But I'll make it up to you later. As much as you want."

"It doesn't matter. I'm right there with you and even it if it's only five seconds, they'll be the best five seconds I've had in a really long time." While she spoke, she hiked the skirt of her dress up and over her hips, bunching it around her waist. "I'll leave the rest up to you," she said with a wink.

Her words fueled him as much as any physical caress and he ripped the flimsy panties from her with one violent tug. The scent of her arousal filled the small space, making Derek's head spin. He gripped her hips and tugged her closer. Fisting his cock in his hand, he brought it to her opening and pushed in with a slow steady stroke.

A long, low groan escaped her as he worked his way inside. She was tight and so fucking hot his eyes nearly crossed. Thank fuck she was soaked, or he would have worried about hurting her.

They both sighed when he sank as deep as he possibly could, but it wasn't enough, not by a long shot.

"Don't hold back," she said. "Don't you dare hold back."

That was all he needed to hear. He drew back then powered into her with a stroke that sent her sliding along the seat. "Yesss," she cried as her hand flew above her head and braced against the door. "More like that. Again."

In the next instant, he was slamming into her with two years' worth of pent-up sexual frustration. His body completely took over, out of his control, no longer under his command. If he'd had any sense, he'd have gentled his hold on her hips, slowed the furious pace of his thrusts and made sure she was as close to exploding as he was, but his mind was blank to everything except the searing pleasure of her pussy.

Sure, the Escalade was roomy, but at six-two, he was a big man, and the back seat wasn't exactly designed for sexual gymnastics. One of his knees dug into the floorboard while the other braced against the seat back.

As predicted, it didn't take long for him to reach the point of no return. He buried himself in her as his surroundings faded away and the pleasure became its own kind of agony. In the distance, he registered the frantic sounds of his woman coming, her body jerking beneath him as she found her release.

He collapsed half on her, half hanging from the seat, in an awkward position, but he'd have lain on a bed of nails if it meant feeling her softness against him.

"Well," she said around heaving breaths. "I think that was actually like twenty seconds. Four times more than you predicted, stud."

He laughed, the jostling motion causing him to slip from her body. He wasn't finished with her, not by a long shot. And if this night wasn't going to end with them tucked away in bed, wrapped around each other while they slept—which he knew it wouldn't—then he was going to get his fill of her before they left his car.

With a muttered curse, he lifted himself off her. Damn, he wasn't a young man anymore. Who'd have thought that at thirty-eight he'd still be able to contort himself enough to fuck a woman to a screaming orgasm in the back of his car? Granted the car was certainly an upgrade from anything he had back in the day, but still. He'd be paying for this tomorrow.

With a huge fuckin' grin on his face.

Kristin lay sprawled on the seat, eyes closed and a satiated smile on her flushed face. While she reveled in the afterglow, he slid two fingers into her soaked channel. Her eyes flew open and a loud gasp flew from her. "Holy shit," she whispered. "What are you doing?"

"No way in hell are we finished, babe." She was completely drenched with the combination of their cum. He curled his fingers, pressing the spot that had her arching into his hand with a whimper. "And while I may need a minute to recover before I can slide back into you, you don't. Keep your eyes open."

"Oh, God." She did as he asked and kept her gorgeous eyes on him.

"You ready?" he asked.

"Yes. No! I don't know. Just don't stop."

He wanted to kiss her, wanted to be further connected to her as he drove her up again, but then he wouldn't have the pleasure of watching her climb.

And it was a fuckin' pleasure.

Chest and face glowing, she gripped the edge of the seat with one hand and the seatbelt with the other, as though she needed an anchor to reality. Her hips rocked, riding his hand and helping to create the perfect friction.

He loved that she wasn't shy about taking what she wanted. Not like this. Not when it was just the two of them. Need for him outweighed her bashful nature. This was a woman who loved touch, loved physical intimacy, loved to come.

"I'm close," she said on a gasp as he worked her with two fingers. Her hips jerked faster, and her eyelids fluttered closed as though she lost the battle to keep them open. He allowed it, too enraptured to care.

With his free hand, he lifted her leg off the seat and ran his tongue along the back of her knee. The unexpected sensation was enough to catapult her over the edge. Her back arched, breasts high and enticing, then she squeezed her eyes tight as she came on a wail.

There wasn't anything in the world more beautiful than watching an orgasm rip through this woman. She gave herself to it fully, basking in every second. Even though it had only been a few minutes and he for damn sure wasn't a man in his twenties, he was rock hard and ready to go again just from watching the show.

He scooped her up and positioned her over his lap, sliding into her with ease. Just inches from his, her eyes widened, and her mouth formed an adorable O shape.

"One more, baby," he said.

"Shit," she whispered, sounding sleepy and satisfied. "I'm not sure I have it in me."

He snorted. She had at least that much in her; he'd put money on it. He slid his hand into the long locks of her hair and guided her mouth toward his. "I need you now," he said.

"Yes," she whispered. "Now." She nodded a fraction of a second before her lips parted and she accepted his kiss. At first, she rode him gently, the soft kiss matching the pace of their lovemaking. But quickly, the fire burned out of control once again. The kiss grew hungrier, tongues clashing, lips pressed together as though trying to permanently fuse and she ground against him with a renewed burst of energy.

She tore her mouth away, sucking in huge gulps of air. Giving in to the madness, she allowed her head to fall back. The end of her hair tickled his thighs and her breasts thrust toward him in an open invitation he'd never decline.

"So good, so good," she chanted, again and again, riding him like he was a wild stallion and she a brave adventurer.

Escapades

There was nothing better in this world than where he was and what he was doing in that moment. Lost in her wet heat, the softness of her plump breast filling his mouth, her cries of joy reaching his ears.

As he raced toward what would no doubt be a devastating orgasm, he was again struck by the magnitude of all he'd been missing out on.

CHAPTER FOUR

Hands on her hips, Alyssa stood on the plush zebra-print area rug in the center of the room. Since the day after Katie passed, the day she retrieved her daughter's favorite dress for the burial, Alyssa hadn't stepped foot in what used to be her favorite room of the house. Funny, considering she'd been dreading taking on nurseries and kids rooms when she started her small interior design business.

It took becoming a mother for her to find joy in creating a warm, playful, and comforting space for a little person. How many hours had she rocked her baby daughter in this very room? How many nights had she kissed Katie's chubby cheeks and wished her sweet dreams? Not enough, that was for sure. But she'd loved every one of those moments.

Now, stepping into the room had been akin to a punch in the stomach. The safari animals painted on the walls mocked her with their toothy grins and large eyes. Toys that had once provided her daughter hours of fun looked sad and forlorn covered in a thick layer of dust. Neglected.

"What was I thinking? I can't do this," Alyssa muttered. She needed to get out of the room before the walls closed in and she suffocated in her grief.

One night. She'd had a one-night vacation from the sadness and despair. The fact that that one night came equipped with more than one mind-melting orgasm was a bonus. A fan-freaking-tastic bonus, but she'd have been almost as happy with just a few sorrow-free hours.

Now, in the light of day, in her house that was once full of life and love, the blissful hours spent with the man known as Jake were overtaken by misery once again.

"Alyssa!" The voice, as familiar as her own, bellowed through the house. "Where the hell are you, chickie?"

Despite her morose mood, the sound of Roxanne's searching yell brought a smile to her face. They were sisters in all but blood and if anyone stood a chance at yanking her out of her depression, it was Roxie.

"Oh, hell no! Do not tell me you are in this room all alone. I just knew you were going to do something stupid today." Roxie appeared in the doorway with her fists on her hips and a severe scowl on her face. Her sleek A-line bob framed the look of disapproval on her face. Her hair was dyed a silver color with streaks of deep purple. It was funky and chic at the same time. Alyssa had always been envious of her friend's easy sense of style and self-confidence. "You just *had* to tackle this today, huh? And alone? Why the hell didn't you wait for your husband to get home from work?"

Because my husband and I don't do things together anymore. A sharp pang of sadness and longing hit her.

"She would have been five today and a half today. I never paid attention to half birthdays until I met you. But since you always took her for ice cream, I remembered." Alyssa picked up the stuffed elephant that had been Katie's constant companion since before she'd turned one. The fur wasn't as soft as it had once been due to countless trips through the washing machine. Sticky hands did quite a number on stuffed animals.

The ache in her heart came from a deep sadness that she couldn't seem to overcome.

"I know, sweetie. That's why I'm here. Why are you doing this today? The room's not going anywhere. You do not have to clean it out today." Roxie sank to her knees on the floor next to Alyssa.

She bent forward and kissed the fuzzy pink elephant Alyssa still held. "Hi, Miss Fuzzy Trunk."

Laughter bubbled out of Alyssa as Roxie used the silly name Katie had given her favorite toy. Leave it to her best friend to get her laughing when seconds before she'd been about to bawl all over the place.

Why was she doing it today? She'd woken up with the sudden realization that she needed to do something drastic to move forward. "It's time, Roxie. I need to do something to shake myself back into the world."

"Okay," Roxie said. "I get that, sweetie, but today? And alone? Again, I ask why you didn't wait for your husband to come home?"

There wasn't much Roxie didn't know about her, but saying the words, "My husband isn't coming home tonight," just wasn't possible.

Alyssa shrugged. "This is the hardest part for me. Being in here. Going through her things. Deciding what to keep and what to let go of. It's like she's dying all over again." Despair swamped her, and she tried in vain to push the heartbreaking memories of her only child's death away. "It's just as hard for him. If we did this together, it would be a disaster. One giant messy grief fest. I need to do it without him." She left out the part where things between her and Derek were not what they once were.

"I get that too. But you don't need to do this alone." She riffled around in the giant handbag that lived on her shoulder, held out her tattoo-covered arms, and presented a bottle. "You have me and Dom for support."

Alyssa laughed again. "Dom? Are you for real? You're telling me you brought a bottle of Dom Perignon?"

"Okay, no I didn't. It's a ten-dollar bottle of some hooch version of champagne. But where's your imagination, chickie?"

Lost. Gone just about a year ago when her daughter finally succumbed to the cancer no child—or parent for that matter—

should ever have to face. God, would it ever stop? Would she ever get to the point where a simple question didn't make her spiral downward?

With a sigh, she tried her hardest not to drown in the heaviness of the past. "Why did you bring champagne?"

Roxie's face grew serious. "Because my goddaughter would have been five and a half today and I refuse to do anything but celebrate her. You know how I feel about half birthdays. They're the shit. And Katie may have only had four short years on this earth, but those four years brought so much light and joy to every person she met. Each of those years deserves to be celebrated. So, hell yes, I brought champagne. And we are going to drink, sort through her things, reminisce, laugh, and yes, probably cry like we're trying to dehydrate ourselves. But the alcohol will numb some of the pain."

Tears were already filling Alyssa's eyes. "God, Roxie. What would I ever do without you?" She was the most remarkable friend. Standing by Alyssa and Derek through all the ups and downs—mostly downs—of Katie's illness. A rock for both of them during the worst hours, of which there were many.

"Please, sweetie, that's something you will never have to find out. All right. I officially call the Celebrate Katie's Life party to order. Woo!" She popped the champagne, sending the cork flying across the room. "Oops."

Alyssa wiped her cheeks dry and smiled at her friend. "So, what's the plan here? We drinking it straight from the bottle?"

"Uh, no." Roxie searched her oversized purse again and drew out two plastic champagne glasses. "We may be sassy but we're still classy, chickie. Now hold up those glasses."

Alyssa laughed so hard the glasses wobbled, and Roxie had a heck of a time filling them.

"Give me that before you're wearing what you should be drinking. This is good shit, after all. Be a shame to waste it." She winked and plopped down on the rug.

Alyssa snorted then held up her plastic flute. She grew serious as she locked eyes with Roxie. "To K-Katie."

"To Katie."

"I miss you every second of every day, baby. Lately, I've been feeling like you're telling me it's time to join the world again. I want you to know I hear you, I'm listening, and I'm going to give it a try. I love you." As she spoke, she ignored the slew of fresh tears and took in the sight of Katie's room for the last time. As her gaze skimmed over the white furniture, the rocking chair, and soft colors of the décor, the strangest sensation overtook her.

A little bit of the sadness flowed away, and a gentle peace settled in her heart. She could do this. This would be good for her. For her and Derek. She couldn't save her relationship with her husband if she was trapped, lost in a world of desolation. And she refused to let her marriage go without a fight.

Suddenly, it felt as though she had Katie's blessing. As though Katie was releasing her from the mourning period and allowing her to live again. Love for her daughter warmed her from the inside out.

Roxie lifted her glass higher and looked toward the heavens. "Damn straight, baby girl. You give your momma the kick in the ass she needs."

"Really, Roxie? She's five. She doesn't need to hear you say damn and she doesn't know what an ass is."

Roxie snorted. "Trust me, with your sailor-turned-tattoo artist husband as her father and me as her favorite auntie, she knows what an ass is."

"Can I finish my toast now?" Alyssa couldn't keep the giggles at bay. God, she loved Roxie and her outrageousness. Her special brand of personality was exactly what Alyssa needed to get through this ordeal in one piece.

"Yes, ma'am. Toast away."

"Thank you. As I was saying..." She frowned. She'd said enough. The rest of her thoughts were private internal thoughts for Katie only. "Well, I guess I was done. I just want her to know I love her and miss her and could never forget her."

"She knows, chickie, she knows." Roxie clinked her glass against Alyssa's. "Rest happy, little angel."

Tears continued to stream as she tilted the glass up for a sip. When she tried to lower it, she was met with the resistance of Roxie's hand on the bottom of her flute. "Drink up, sweetie. The next few hours have the potential to suck. We need to lube up a bit."

Lube up? Alyssa nearly shot the cheap champagne out of her nose she laughed so hard. But she understood Roxie's reasoning.

Two hours, a bottle and a half of champagne, many rounds of laughter, and about a gallon of tears later, the two sprawled on the floor with their backs against Katie's twin bed. Three large piles rested in different corners of the room. A keep pile, a donate pile, and a toss pile.

It was over.

Done.

Everything her daughter had owned had been sorted through.

Roxie was right. It wasn't something Alyssa should have ever attempted on her own. Not only would it have taken twice as long, but it would have been a horrible depressing experience. With Roxie, it was cathartic.

"Thanks, hon," she said resting her head on Roxie's inked shoulder.

"I wouldn't have been anywhere else. Can I ask you something and blame it on the alcohol?"

Alyssa straightened, and the room did a little flip-flop. Whoops. Perhaps too much champagne. Not that it mattered. She had nowhere to go that night but bed. "Anything."

"Things getting any better with Derek?"

Gloom threatened to kill her buzz and for a moment she almost played it off and acted like things were wonderful. But, while Roxie may be outrageous and the opposite of Alyssa's more reserved personality, she was no dummy. She'd been not so subtly dropping hints that she sensed their marriage was on unsteady ground for months.

With a shake of her head, Alyssa sighed. "Not really. Not since...you know. Things are just...different. Not bad. We don't fight, we don't yell, we don't have any ill feelings toward each other. Things have just changed. Neither of us is who we were before Katie got sick. It's like we've forgotten how to be together. If that makes any sense." She'd give anything to get the closeness, both emotionally and physically, of her marriage back. The rapid wasting away of the intense intimacy they'd shared was almost as devastating as her daughter's passing.

"You having sex?"

"Roxie!"

"Oh please, girlfriend. I know you don't like to talk about sex, even with me. I blame your crazy conservative parents for that one."

Alyssa laughed. "Well, my father is a minister."

Roxie waved her champagne. "Yeah, yeah. And you know it's more a cult than a church. Anyway, I know you and I know that man of yours. You may talk like a prude, but you two have one hell of a wild and crazy sex life."

Alyssa's face burned. "What? How...how would you even know something like that?" It was the truth, but as Roxie said, she never talked about it with anyone beyond Derek.

With a snort, Roxie threw back the last of her drink. "Sweetie, not only did we share an apartment when you and Derek first started dating, we shared a freakin' wall. I heard things that still fuel my wet dreams."

"Oh my God." She buried her face. Hell, she would have crawled under Katie's bed and hidden like her daughter once tried to do during a thunderstorm if she wasn't certain Roxie would drag her out by her ankles and make her share the dirty deets anyway.

Tipsy laughter filled the air. "Don't be embarrassed, sweetie. Own that shit. You should be saying, 'hell yeah I have a man who gives it to me so good I scream down the house.'"

"Well, I had that anyway." Okay, she still had it if the events in the car a few nights ago were any indication, but it was on shaky ground. She drew up her knees and dropped her forehead down. The soothing, if not slightly uncoordinated and intoxicated rub of Roxie's hand over her back comforted her.

"You check out that therapist I recommended?"

"You mean that therapist whose phone number magically appeared on a slip of paper in my purse? You're about a subtle as a hand grenade, Rox." Alyssa's face heated and she turned her head, resting her cheek on her bent knees. "Um, yeah, I checked her out. Her methods are certainly…unorthodox."

Roxie laughed and nudged Alyssa with her shoulder. "But good stuff, huh?" She winked "You gonna call her?"

Geez, could her face get any hotter? She often wondered if she wouldn't be so skittish when it came to talking about sex if she hadn't had such a strict religious upbringing. Hell, she hadn't even heard the phrase blow job until she was seventeen. Slightly late by today's standards. "We've already been to see her."

Face alight with happiness, Roxie squealed. "Well, damn, girl," she said. Then she snickered. "The session must have been torture for you."

"You have no idea. It required me to talk about more details than I ever thought I'd share, but it's…good. I think it might work. I can't lose him too, Rox. I wouldn't survive it. I'm barely making it through the day as things are now. If they were to end…" Her breathing hitched, and she shook her head.

"Hey." Roxie's voice hardened. Alyssa liked to call it her teacher voice. "There is no way that would ever happen. For two reasons. One, because that man is fucking insane over you and he'd rather get a butterfly tattoo on his face than lose you. And two, because I'd kick his ass across the Atlantic if he ever tried to leave." She huffed and rose to her feet, pulling Alyssa along with her. "Okay, enough serious stuff. Time to get out of here and put something besides bubbly alcohol in our bellies. Then you can give me all the filthy details of your assignment from the therapist. I have to live vicariously through your sex life."

"Please, Roxie, you know you're hot. And you have a boyfriend." She frowned. "You and Gregg have to be hitting the sheets every chance you get. Aren't you?"

A grunt came from Roxie. "Please, girl. You know I'm a test drive the car kinda girl. He's just a bit more concerned with himself lately if you know what I mean. And I'm starting to think his face is too smooth."

Alyssa stopped her friend with a hand on her shoulder. This was the first time Roxie had ever uttered a negative word about her boyfriend of six months. "His face is too smooth?" She snorted out a laugh. "Wanna elaborate on that one?"

"Don't laugh. You got yourself a bearded man. All dark hair, dark eyes, rugged man." Roxie shook her head and waved off Alyssa's concern. "Ignore me, everything's fine. Just being silly."

Hmm. For now, she'd respect Roxie's wishes. After the emotional roller coaster of the past few hours, they didn't need to dive into another taxing conversation. Honestly, she'd been surprised when Roxie started dating Gregg of the two G variety. He was very clean cut, sophisticated to the point of snobby. Not like any of the men Rox had dated in the past. She tended to gravitate toward more of a bad boy.

Roxie wasn't one to put up with nonsense from a man. Nor was she the type to stick with a guy who didn't rock her world, so to speak. Alyssa filed it away for the time being but planned to bring it up again soon.

Alyssa reached for her friend and drew her into a suffocating hug. "Love you, Roxie," she whispered. "Thank you."

"Nothing to thank me for, sweetie," Roxie said, returning the embrace. "You've done so much for me in the past. And I love you too."

The room wavered a bit, but the woozy feeling wasn't unpleasant. In fact, it was nice. A strong buzz and her best friend made the afternoon she'd been dreading for almost a year bearable and she'd be forever grateful for both.

If only someone could make all the painful memories of the past two years disappear, starting with the day they learned of Katie's illness. And while they were at it, maybe they could glue her marriage back together. And add some duct tape for good measure.

Then, maybe she could make it through the day without the ache in her chest.

CHAPTER FIVE

Two years ago

Alyssa's foot tapped a rapid rhythm on the threadbare carpet while all ten chewed fingernails drummed on the wooden armrest of the waiting room chair. For the past two days, she'd had a tornado of stress and worry spiraling in her mind.

She filled her cheeks with air and blew out a long, slow breath.

Five after ten.

Their appointment was ten o'clock. What was taking so long? There should really be some sort of law against physicians running late when life-altering information hung in the balance.

Derek's warm palm slid over her hand, stilling the incessant movement. "Baby, relax," he said. "Everything is going to be fine. You know what Dr. Oakes said. This is just a precaution. Covering all their bases. He even admitted it was probably overkill."

No one was better under pressure than Derek. Probably came from ten years in the Navy, six spent as a SEAL. Couldn't have hacked it in Special Forces if he'd been prone to panicking in high-stress situations. Even though it had been years since he left the Navy, that calm, coolness in the face of...well, anything, stuck with him.

Alyssa on the other hand? Well, she was practically crawling out of her skin.

She flipped her hand over and interlaced their fingers. The other hand, though, still fidgeted like it was attached to a live wire.

"Mr. and Mrs. Jackson, come on back to my office." Dr. Oakes hovered in the doorway that led from the waiting area to offices and treatment rooms. Older than her by at least twenty-five years, the physician had a grandfatherly look about him. Gray hair, twinkling eyes, kind smile.

Children warmed to him in an instant, even when they knew he was the one giving out shots. There was just a comforting way about him. He'd really found his calling as a pediatrician.

Why was Dr. Oakes himself the one coming out to the waiting room to fetch them? Wasn't that the medical assistant's job? Did that mean he had bad news? Or was the assistant just busy? Could it be he came out himself because the news was good, and he didn't want them to stress unnecessarily?

"Come on, Katie bug." Derek clasped their three-year-old daughter's hand as their little family headed toward the doctor.

This had to be what some poor prisoner felt like when a pirate made them walk the plank. One foot in front of the other until the end appeared. Then, nowhere to go but down, down, down to a swirling sea of horrors.

Geez, the negative thinking needed to stop, but controlling the obsessive thoughts wasn't easy.

She was going to make herself sick.

"Breathe, babe," Derek said as though he could sense her racing thoughts. His dark gaze held hers, strong and steady.

"Well, hey there, Katie," Dr. Oakes said, crouching and giving their little towhead a playful tug on her pigtail. She'd been all about the pigtails over the past few weeks, insisting on wearing her hair in the style every moment of every day. She'd even begged to sleep in them and it was a battle Alyssa didn't feel was worth fighting so she'd allowed it.

"Hi, Dr. Oates," Katie said with a sunny smile.

Alyssa smiled herself. That darn K sound tripped their daughter up every time. Even her own name came out as Tatie.

"Do you and your parents want to come with me for a bit? I've got some toys you can play with down the hall."

"Yes! Can we, mommy? Can we?" The high level of enthusiasm their three-year-old displayed over any and everything never failed to amuse her and Derek. It was as though she was offered a trip to Disney instead of a walk down the hall.

"Sure thing, sweetie. Just follow Dr. Oakes."

Katie bounded after the doctor with her and Derek only a few steps behind.

"I'm going to let her play in this room here," Dr. Oakes said as he paused outside a small playroom. "There's plenty to keep her busy and Melissa, one of my nurses will stay with her the whole time."

Oh God. He didn't want Katie in the room. That could only mean one thing.

"Go right on in and play, sweetie," he said to Katie. "I'm going to talk to your mom and dad for a bit. You can stay in here, so you don't get bored listening to all the grown-up talk." He said the words as though grown-up talk had a disgusting flavor to it.

Katie giggled. Okay, so he didn't want her bored. That could mean the news wasn't horrible. Jesus, she was going crazy.

He turned to her and Derek. "My office is just here, next door, and there's a large widow so you can see her playing."

With a wave for Katie and the older nurse, they followed him into the next room.

"Have a seat, please," Dr. Oakes said as they entered the small office. There wasn't anything special about the space. Just a desk, two chairs, and bookshelf littered with medical texts and journals.

Alyssa's decorator's eye cringed at the white walls devoid of anything save for a few framed diplomas and a medical license.

The workspace needed a good revamp. It should be colorful and playful, especially since children were often around.

Shaking herself back to the moment, she sat and waited for Derek to join her. She tried to concentrate on steadying the in and out of her breathing when what she really wanted to do was lunge across the desk and shake the doctor until he gave them promising news.

Once all three adults were seated and Katie was playing with blocks next door and blissfully unaware that those adults were discussing her, Dr. Oakes began.

"So, how's Katie feeling today?" he asked.

Ugh. Alyssa just wanted him to get straight to it. Though it had only been two days since the bone marrow biopsy, it felt like an eternity and another few seconds of uncertainty seemed impossible to endure.

"Pretty well," Derek said. "No fever today. She ate a little more breakfast and is just a little sore from the procedure."

Dr. Oakes nodded and shuffled through a haphazard pile of papers on his desk. Alyssa stared at him, hard, dissecting his features for any indication of how this meeting was going to play out.

Did that wrinkle between his eyes mean he had bad news?

Wait, a smile. That had to be positive, right?

He scratched his chin. What could that mean?

Derek squeezed her hand. He was so in tune with her. She sent him a grateful smile and returned the grip. She loved the man more than she ever thought it was possible to love someone.

"Good to hear." Dr. Oakes said. "So, just to review, my main concerns with Katie were the nausea and weight loss, fatigue, and fevers. Usually, these symptoms are associated with either viral or bacterial infections. We become concerned, however, when the symptoms do not respond to treatment as has been the case with Katie. Combine that with the easy bruising you're reporting, and the nosebleeds, and it was time to start digging a bit deeper, hence the bone marrow biopsy."

He sighed. A long, troubled, deep sigh. Then he raised his head and stared straight into her eyes.

Alyssa's stomach plummeted straight to the floor. In that instant, she knew what was coming and had the strong and juvenile urge to close her eyes, plug her ears and scream, "la la la," at the top of her lungs.

"There's no easy way to say this, so I'm just going to give it to you straight."

No. No, no, no.

Derek's hold on her hand tightened to the point of painful, but she didn't object. It was the only thing keeping her from flying out of the seat and running away from reality.

"Katie's official diagnosis is Acute Lymphocytic Leukemia."

A low buzzing started in Alyssa's ears and increased in volume until it drowned out the rest of the doctor's words. The medical world was a mystery to her, but she knew the word leukemia meant cancer. And she knew cancer was bad. As in worst case scenario bad.

Oh God. Not my baby.

Not her perfect, innocent baby girl with the blond pigtails. She stared at her daughter through the glass. Oblivious to the conversation, Katie giggled as her tower of blocks grew too high and toppled.

An impending sob clawed at her throat, but she somehow forced it down. Later, she could lose it. Later, she could rage and cry until her eyes felt like sandpaper and her throat was raw. But not now. Not in front of Katie.

Through the roaring in her ears, she caught words like oncologist, chemotherapy, hospitalization and for a few moments, she worried she'd throw up. She should have questions. Hundreds of questions. But nothing came. Her brain couldn't process the words being said. After an unknown amount of time, she felt a gentle tug on her arm.

Escapades

Derek was standing next to her chair, one hand on her upper back and one cupping her elbow. She blinked. Apparently, the meeting was over. Rising with robotic, jerky movements, she nodded to the doctor whose face was sad and sympathetic. Then she turned and followed Derek out of the office.

Thank God, her brain seemed to a have an automatic mode because she couldn't have functioned otherwise.

Left foot. Right foot. Her muscles triggered of their own accord, guiding her to the exit.

"Are you okay, Mommy?" Katie slipped her hand into Alyssa's and peered up while they walked toward the car. Her little forehead was furrowed and eyes wide. "You look sad. Don't be sad, mommy. I love you."

The ache those few sweet words caused was nearly crushing in its force. Alyssa swallowed her despair and smiled the biggest smile she could muster. Which was probably only a fraction of what she usually gifted her daughter. But it was better than nothing. There was no way she'd let her daughter know how distraught she was.

So, she pulled herself together and scooped Katie up, carrying her the rest of the way toward the car. Derek slipped his arm around her waist. His presence helped bolster her and provided the strength she needed to be positive for Katie. "I'm great, sweetie. Are you excited to go out to lunch with Aunt Roxie?"

"Yes!" Katie said. "I want chiten nuggets."

Derek ruffled her hair. "I'm sure Aunt Roxie will get you whatever you want, bug. She always spoils you." He buckled Katie into her car seat, shut the door, then cupped Alyssa's face.

"Fifteen minutes, babe. Just have to hold it together for fifteen more minutes, then you can lose it. Okay?"

"O-okay."

About twenty seconds after they parked in their driveway, Roxie's Toyota pulled in behind them. As soon as she was unbuckled, Katie ran to greet her and climbed right into Roxie's car. Roxie had purchased a car seat before Katie was even born.

She'd been almost as excited as Alyssa and Derek for the little girl they'd be bringing into the world. Since day one, she'd spent a ton of time with her goddaughter.

"Hey, you okay?" Roxie asked.

"Um, yeah. I'm good," Alyssa said in what she was sure was a totally unconvincing voice. "Headache."

Roxie narrowed her eyes. "Okay, if you say so. I'll bring her back in a few hours. Have fun, you two crazy kids." She winked and slipped into her car, driving off with a cheerful wave.

"Come on, Lyss. Let's go in the house."

The moment the door closed, Alyssa said, "It's my fault. My punishment for all my sins, Derek. For turning away from my family. For barely speaking to them."

He gripped her face between his rough hands and looked her straight in the eye. "Lyss, stop. That's not true and you damn well know it. That's your father talking. And it's garbage. You're just freaking out and not thinking clearly."

He was right. No one had caused this. It was just horrible luck —or unluck—of the draw.

Suddenly the magnitude of what they were about to face hit her with a powerful force. The fear, pain, and helplessness were crushing. It was as though the air itself had weight to it and pressed into her from all angles, hard enough to grind her to dust.

Her forehead dropped to Derek's chest and she lost the battle to remain stoic. Giant tears fell from her eyes and she cried the ugliest cry she could ever remember crying. Derek's arms banded around her, and he held her close through the full-body sobs. He whispered to her, stroked her hair, and rocked her back and forth right there in their foyer. The soft brush of his beard against her cheek and the familiar scent of beard oil comforted her more than any words could have.

When she finally calmed, she looked up at him. His eyes were glassy and his face as tragic as hers had to be. Immediately, the heavy weight of shame and selfishness pressed down on her shoulders. Here he was, comforting her when Katie was his daughter too, and he had to be as wrecked as she was.

"What are we going to do, Der?" she asked, her throat ravaged from the crying jag.

"The only thing we can do, baby. Fight like hell. She's a tough kiddo. She's gonna kick this in the ass. And we'll be right by her side every step of the way."

She was a tough kid, they were by her side every step of the way, and they'd fought it with every weapon in their specialist's arsenal. But it hadn't worked, and after months of grueling treatment, the oncologist gave them the news that came with a pain so great Alyssa couldn't breathe.

The treatment wasn't working. Ineffective was the word he'd used. Still made her sick to her stomach every time she heard that word.

Her baby wasn't going to make it.

In the privacy of her room, she'd railed and screamed and shed so many tears she could have filled a pool, but in front of Katie, she'd always tried to put on a happy face.

They'd lost the battle.

A little piece of her heart died right alongside her only child.

CHAPTER SIX

Derek smiled as the buzz of the tattoo machine filled the near-empty shop. Seven thirty on Tuesday morning, an hour and a half before his shop opened, and the only occupants of the eclectic space were him and his client, Hunter.

Six months ago, Hunter had been medically discharged from the Navy after an IED took one of his legs, just below the knee, as well as one arm halfway between his elbow and wrist. Physically, the man was a beast and adapted to his prosthetic limbs faster and with more proficiency than anyone Derek had seen. Unfortunately, as for most injured vets, the physical healing was only half the battle, maybe less than half.

Loud or crowded spaces were challenging for Hunter who was battling a wicked case of PTSD. Something Derek knew about all too well. Since Trident Ink tended to blast pulsing music and be full of large, gruff and raucous clients as well as staff during working hours, Derek was more than willing to accommodate Hunter and was working on the man during the off hours.

It was one of his best pieces yet if he did say so himself. He'd been inking it for over two months, and a few more sessions should do it. From the tip of his shoulder to the end of Hunter's limb, where the amputation had taken place, Derek was transforming the skin, some smooth and some scarred, into the inner working of a cyborg. Gears, nuts, bolts, wires, metallic colors, the whole shebang. It was badass and would look amazing when paired with Hunter's top-of-the-line prosthesis.

Reclined in the chair, arm stretched out on a table, Hunter's eyes were closed and earbuds in. Confident that his client was tolerating the needle without too much discomfort or needing a break, Derek lost himself converting Hunter's arm to a work of art.

After a while, his lower back began to twinge, so Derek switched off the machine and wiped dots of blood from Hunter's skin.

"Shit, man, that's sick." Derek jumped when Brett, his business partner and piercer extraordinaire spoke over his shoulder. Thank God Brett had held off on the sneak attack until he was through inking Hunter's skin.

"Geez, bro, what the hell are you creeping up on me like that for? You know I'd have to kill you if you fucked up Hunter's ink."

Brett smiled a shit-eating grin and lifted a hand in greeting to Hunter as he strode across the shop. "I couldn't resist. You were so far gone into the zone you had no idea I've been here for twenty minutes. It's getting close to opening time, thought you might want to wrap it up with him. And I purposely waited until I was sure you were shut down. I don't have a death wish."

With a grunt, Derek set about bandaging his client's fresh ink. Hunter pulled out his earbuds and said a quick greeting to Brett who was scanning the appointment scheduler on the computer behind the reception desk. There were still a good fifteen minutes before they officially opened, and it was unusual for Brett to be in any earlier than one minute before go time. Typically, he rolled out of whatever woman's bed he'd spent the night in ten minutes before his first client, left her without a word, and hightailed it to the shop.

"How's it looking?" Hunter asked, breaking Derek out of his thoughts.

He couldn't help the giant grin that spread across his face. "Damn good, brother. If we push it, I might be able to get it completed in the next session, if not, two more max."

"Sweet," Hunter said as he swung his legs around and sat sideways on the reclining chair.

"Let me grab you something to drink. Sit for a minute."

Hunter gave him a mock salute. "I know the drill, LT."

Derek jogged toward the refrigerator and grabbed Brett a bottle of juice. "You need me to review the aftercare?" he asked, handing over the beverage.

"Nah, I'm good. Been through it enough times lately." It was their fifth session, working about three hours at a time.

"All right, man. I'll have Trish call you to make an appointment when she gets in."

"Sounds good, Derek. Thanks. Appreciate you adjusting your hours for me."

Derek waved it off. "Ain't a thing, bro."

They shook hands then Hunter headed out, calling, "See ya, Brett," as he passed the reception desk.

"Later," Brett answered.

Derek began the process of breaking down his equipment and loading the autoclave which would sterilize everything. He could do it in his sleep and finished in no time, which meant he had a few spare minutes to grab a cup of coffee before his first official client rolled in.

He spun toward the coffee machine and stopped in his tracks when he took in the amused look on Brett's face. "What? Something in my teeth?"

"Ha, no." Brett laughed. "You look good today, man. In fact, you've seemed different the past few days. Relaxed. Dare I say happy? Been a while."

Both statements were true. He was more relaxed, happier. Sure, it had been four days since his erotic date with *Kristin*, but the memories still played through his mind and had powered him through the days with a positive outlook. Something that had been absent from his life for too long.

"Yeah, I've been feeling pretty good lately. Coffee?"

"Shit, yes," Brett said in a reverent tone. "Haven't had any yet this morning."

"Aww, what happened? Your nightly conquest didn't offer you a pancake breakfast and homemade cappuccino?" The smell of freshly brewed coffee filled the shop as he filled two cups.

Brett snorted. "No, she did not," he said, unabashed as he accepted the cup of coffee Derek handed him. He upended the sugar and let the sweet crystals pour into the cup. "I didn't mean to stay until morning, but I passed out. She got a little miffed when I called her by the wrong name this morning." He shrugged and sipped what had to be crazy-sweet coffee. "Ahh, good stuff."

Derek could practically feel a toothache forming just watching Brett drink the sugar-loaded beverage. "Ugh, I don't know how you can drink it like that. Especially that mocha crap you get from Farhad. You're a SEAL for Christ's sake. Black's the only way to go, my friend."

Farhad was an elderly middle-eastern gentleman who owned a convenience store down the block from Trident Ink. He sold great coffee, and Brett lived off these sugary mocha latte things he sold.

Brett tossed his head back and let out a loud laugh. "That's exactly why I drink it like this. Way too many years of sludge and instant coffee. Now I can and do doctor it the hell up."

"How's Farhad doing by the way?" Brett asked. "I haven't been in for my usual in way too long."

Derek and Farhad had struck up a bit of a friendship. His wife was currently undergoing chemotherapy for leukemia. Not the same kind Katie had, but his wife was just as sick as she'd been. It was a true struggle for the older man and Derek could relate to the pain of watching a loved one suffer with the terrible disease.

"Talked to him yesterday. Things are tough. Money is tight. She's always feeling like shit and he's away a lot keeping the store running. They have a good family though."

Brett shook his head. "Fuckin' cancer."

"You said it."

He slapped Derek on the back. "Damn, man, I gotta say it's good to see you smiling and joking this morning. Bagging on me about my superb taste in coffee. Been a while. Things getting better between you and Alyssa?"

With a cough, Derek almost spewed his coffee across the room. Better with him and Alyssa? What the hell? Sure, he and Alyssa knew their marriage was on shaky ground, but...their friends noticed it too? He'd never mentioned a word of it to Brett. "What do you mean? Things are fine with us."

His buddy set down his coffee and crossed his arms over his wide chest. In some regards, he and Brett had a similar look. Tall, broad-shouldered, bearded, muscular without being overly bulky. But the similarities ended there. Where Derek was dark, Brett was light, with sandy hair, hazel eyes, and a much blonder beard.

A few times, Alyssa had compared him to Charlie Hunnam and boy did that go straight to Brett's already too big head. He'd strutted around for months using the description shamelessly to bed women. The man was truly a slut.

One light eyebrow rose, and Brett remained silent, shooting Derek a you're-full-of-shit look.

"What?"

"Come on, D. We may not be touchy-feely, vomit-your-emotions guys, but we're usually straight with each other. Anyone with eyes can see things have deteriorated between you and Alyssa since...well in the last year or so. I haven't seen you fight or anything, but I also haven't seen you together. In ages. You stopped coming out together and stopped hosting Sunday brunch. You've been doing that shit every Sunday for what, six years?"

Another denial was on the tip of his tongue, but Brett knew him too well to buy any bullshit coming from his mouth. They'd been friends going on eighteen years, ever since they were paired as swim buddies in BUDS, the hellacious training all SEALS suffered through. Those experiences, plus years of being on the same SEAL team forged an unbreakable bond. It was only natural they'd go into business together when they separated from the military.

But, close as they were, they didn't really delve into their emotions. Derek didn't do that with anyone…well, he did with Alyssa. Christ, he missed his wife. Missed their closeness. Missed talking to her, missed holding her, missed sharing their days, and smelling her, tasting her, feeling her come all over him. What would it hurt to let Brett in on what was happening? Apparently, he wasn't doing a good job at hiding it anyway.

"I don't know, man." He sighed and forced himself to say the two words he'd not allowed past his lips in over a year. "Katie's death—" He cleared his suddenly thick throat. "Ah, Katie's death really put a few cracks in our foundation. Maybe it's been all on me. I don't know." He ran a hand through his hair.

"Derek," Brett said. "What you guys went through is unimaginable for people who have never experienced it. Cracks in your foundation? Hell, you guys are winning the race if you just have a few cracks. There's a reason more than half of couples dissolve after the death of a child. It's fucking devastating."

More than half? Damn, that was some pretty bad odds. "How do you know that?"

Color rose in Brett's cheeks as he shrugged. "I've been reading up. We've survived some serious shit together in the past. I'll always have your back, you know that. Thought maybe I could help you guys out."

As though a light bulb flicked on in his head, Derek realized just how disconnected from life he'd been since Katie got sick. Not only had he drifted from his wife, but he'd distanced himself from his friends as well. Words Alyssa said in a conversation a week ago came rushing back to him. *I feel like I'm finally waking up after a two-year-long nightmare.* Maybe it was time for him to get his head out of his ass and wake up as well.

"I guess I've kinda been operating in this detached autopilot mode for the past couple of years, just mindlessly plowing through. Working on it though. Can't fuckin' lose Alyssa."

"That's good, bro. Real good. And I don't want to pry into your private life with Alyssa, but I think if anyone has what it takes to make it through the shit times, it's you two."

"Thanks, man."

"You guys are the one couple that's kept me from completely writing off the idea of a relationship. So don't fuck it up. Otherwise, you'll be ruining it for me as well as yourself."

Derek laughed. Leave it to Brett to bring them back to busting each other's balls. "I'll do my best not to let you down."

"See that you don't," Derek said as the bells jangled over the entrance, indicating their receptionist, Trish's, arrival. Trailing their employee was Brett's first client, a gorgeous twenty-something student who would most likely get more than just a navel piercing from Brett. "Ahh, best get to it. Lady's waiting to be poked with my long tool." He waggled his eyebrows up and down.

"Shit," Derek said. "If I had a buck for every time you told that awful joke, I could retire and move to Hawaii."

A middle finger was all the response he received.

Brett had the co-ed giggling, rubbing her silicone chest against his arm, and batting her long lashes at him in seconds. Jealousy burned hot in Derek's gut. Not that he had any interest in the girl—or any woman besides his wife for that matter—but he missed the flirty banter, come-hither glances, and building anticipation that eventually led to mind blowing nights. Something that had never faded between him and Alyssa despite years of marriage, a child, job stress…

And it still hadn't faded. He almost wished it had. No, it disappeared completely and faster than a whore spread her legs.

Escapades

It was time to give himself a kick in his own ass. There was no reason to gawk in envy at his man-whore of a best friend while he had a hot, sexy woman at home who still got him hard as steel with just a look.

He'd do anything to fix what was broken between them. No matter how skeptical he'd been of the plan at first. After the passionate night he shared with his wife four days ago, he was all in. Ready to do what it took to repair his marriage. Especially if it meant he got to see her come like she had in his car.

CHAPTER SEVEN

Alyssa tapped the key card against her palm and glanced down the hall toward the bank of elevators. Had she timed it wrong? A quick glance at her phone confirmed it was six twenty in the evening. Timing was right.

Then where the hell was he?

People were going to start wondering why she'd been loitering in the hallway outside the hotel suite for the past fifteen minutes.

Maybe she should leave.

Maybe this was a mistake.

Too ridiculous. Too out of the box. Okay, so no one had actually walked past since she'd arrived. She was freaking out for nothing. But she was freaking out. It was so stupid. She wasn't doing anything wrong. No reason to be a nervous Nellie.

An elevator dinged, and her heart leaped into her throat as she got into position. If it wasn't him emerging from the elevator, she'd look like a moron, but that was a risk she was willing to take. Because if this played out the way she hoped, she'd be going home with a smile on her face and a little pep in her step. Plus, she'd be one step closer to where she wanted to be. Where she wanted them to be.

She flipped the keycard around and inserted it into the door slot, backward. As expected, a red light flashed on the panel indicating non-acceptance of the key. With a huffy sigh, she did it again, then again.

"Damn it," she muttered. Drawing in a breath of courage, she turned and met the newcomer head on. "Excuse me," she said with more confidence than she was feeling. "Do you think you could give me a hand for a moment?"

And there he was.

Really, she'd known without looking. His energy called to her and a zing of awareness shot across her skin the moment the elevator bell chimed. God, he was handsome. The years had only made him more appealing. The full, but closely cropped dark beard covering his face was her absolute favorite feature. She would truly mourn if he ever shaved it off. Just the sight of it made her shiver with the desire to feel those soft hairs tickling her breasts, her stomach, her inner thighs.

He was so strong. Both in character and in the brawny-man sense. Each of those traits appealed to her, but she couldn't deny the initial spark of physical awareness he'd ignited in her from the first time she'd laid eyes on him. The slight scowl he'd worn back then combined with the bulging muscles made an intriguing and formidable picture. And that was all before finding out he could kill a man six ways, with just his pinkie toe.

Despite the menacing look about him, he'd never intimidated Alyssa. Okay, that was a lie. Once she got to know him, he didn't seem intimidating. When they'd first met she'd been a strange mix of intrigued, aroused, and terrified all at the same time. But the man had a soft side a mile wide—for her anyway.

His gaze landed on her and for one step, his gait hitched. Then a sinful smile curled his talented lips and he stopped about two feet from her. "Yes, ma'am. What can I help you with?"

Wetness trickled down the inside of those thighs from thoughts of what could happen in the next few minutes. Maybe leaving off the panties hadn't been as good of an idea as she originally thought.

She stepped close enough that his intoxicating scent of leather, cologne, and man surrounded her. Close enough to brush the tips of her breasts against his firm bicep. Then she held up the keycard.

Her nipples hardened, visible through the silk blouse she wore. Not surprising since her bra was little more than a thin layer of lace. "My keycard doesn't seem to be working. I've been trying to get into my room for the past five minutes with no luck. Mind giving it a whirl before I have to trek all the way down to the front desk in these shoes?"

His gaze started at the four-inch peep-toe heels, traveled up her bare calves, skimmed over her rounded hips, then lingered on her exposed cleavage. He raised an eyebrow and one side of his mouth twitched. The chances of him buying that lame story were slim, but at least he seemed willing to play along. "My pleasure, gorgeous."

"Thank you."

He overshot his reach, wrapped his hand around her wrist, and slowly stroked callused fingers across her skin as he relieved her of the key.

A dead woman would have risen from her coffin for more of that touch. There was something about the brush of a man's coarse touch grazing over her sensitive skin that was almost unbearably erotic.

Not any man's touch, just this man's. Goosebumps erupted up and down her arms with just the five-second caress.

Once he had the key, he glided it into the lock—in the correct direction, of course—and was rewarded with the green light and snick of the unlocking door.

"Looks like you have the magic touch." She winked as she opened the door and sashayed into the room. Spinning on one pointed heel, she faced him and held the door. "I'm Quinn, by the way. Care to come in for a thank you drink?" she asked, gesturing into the room. "It's the least I can do."

He stared at her face, his playful gaze heating her cheeks. Then, he took another slow tour of her body, and his expression went from teasing to smoldering in an instant. She'd worn a tailored shirt and kept the top two buttons open, revealing a hint of cleavage. Just enough catch and sustain his interest.

"It's Tyler, and, yeah, I could use a drink," he said as he strode into the room, muscles flexing and playing with each step.

She almost laughed out loud. The name Tyler was a longstanding joke between them. She'd once told him it was her favorite hot guy name. Ever since, he'd teased her about hiding a man named Tyler in their closet and letting him out when he wasn't home.

Alyssa was as helpless to tear her attention from his body as he seemed to be from hers. "Scotch okay?" she asked, making her way to the small island that separated the living area from the en suite kitchenette. Two barstools rested in front of the island and she stepped between them, reaching for the bottle of Scotch she'd left in the room earlier.

"Scotch is perfect."

"Great." Her hands trembled slightly as she poured two glasses and recapped the bottle. He was close when she turned and held out the drink. It took a few seconds for his focus to rise to her face as his attention had clearly been on her ass while she prepared the drinks.

Darkened with lust, his leather-brown gaze bore into hers, stealing her breath. After pressing the glass into his hand, she lightly tapped her tumbler against his. "Cheers. To Good Samaritans, willing to help a random damsel in distress."

A quick chuckle was all the reaction she received before he tossed his head back and downed his drink in one large gulp, his throat working with the force of his swallow. Then, he closed the gap between them, standing so close his Scotch-scented breath wafted across her cheek. "Drink up." His voice was gravelly, dark, and rough, and she shivered in response.

So far, the encounter was playing out exactly as planned.

With a shake of her head, she handed her tumbler to him and he downed it as well before stalking closer to her. She didn't want anything to dull this experience. Large hands landed on the marble countertop, on either side of her, pinning her to the island. She tilted her head up to see his face, and another quiver of anticipation rippled through her. What came next would be the stuff fantasies were made of; she'd put money on it.

"That skirt should be illegal," he practically growled down at her. "It makes a man think very dirty thoughts."

"Those are the best kind of thoughts." The flirty back and forth was a blast and reminded her of how they used to be. It was about to get even better if the bulge behind his dark jeans was any indication.

She'd worn a curve-hugging pencil skirt. The kind that was so snug, it hindered her stride when she walked but did amazing things for her ass. Nice to know the effort hadn't gone unnoticed.

"I'm not sure one drink is a sufficient thank you. I had things to do this evening. Maybe you should offer something else, to make up for screwing with my plans." As he spoke, his large hands slipped under the hem of her skirt and began to work the close-fitting material up her thighs.

His hands were warm, callused, and strong as they slid over her flesh. God, she loved this. The slow seduction, the buildup that made her crazy with want. Her mind swam with delicious sensations, making a response difficult. "Um…did you have something specific in mind?" she managed to ask.

"Your pussy," he said, and she gasped. Without the barrier of panties, she was embarrassingly wet. Her thighs were soaked with evidence of how his words and touch affected her.

Tyler's hands finally reached her hips and he spread them over the globes of her ass. The skirt was bunched around her waist leaving her skin exposed to the air, his gaze, his touch, whatever he wanted. "Fuck. You're not wearing panties," he stated as he squeezed her ass.

"Nope," she said with a sassy grin.

"Fuck me. I need to see. Right now." Without any warning, he lifted her and plopped her down on the island. When her bare ass landed on the cold marble and she squeaked out a small protest. "Changed my mind. I'll look in a minute. This first," he said, his voice thick with need.

He cupped the back of her neck and kissed her with what felt like years of denied need and desire. All she could do was keep her head tipped back and surrender to his savage claiming. While he stole her senses with his mouth, he yanked at the pins securing her hair. They scattered around the kitchenette and her hair tumbled down her back. After he finished wrecking her hair, he moved on to her shirt.

The crushing pressure of his mouth moving against hers felt so good, so right. He tasted of Scotch and she bit his lower lip, sucking it into her mouth as he let out a groan. "Enough," he said, ripping away.

They stared at each other, chests heaving. Her blouse was now untucked from the waistband of her gathered skirt, and all the buttons had been popped open. He gazed at her lace-covered breasts with a hungry glare. "Time for my thank you."

One rough hand scooped under her thigh and lifted, placing her heeled foot on the barstool. As he repeated the action with her other leg, she was forced to brace her hands on the countertop behind her. Either that or tumble back due to the angle the position demanded. Her legs were bent at the knees and splayed open with a foot on each of the barstools, baring her sex to Tyler's ravenous gaze.

"Lean back on your elbows," he ordered without looking away from her drenched sex.

Ignoring his command wasn't even a thought and she immediately complied. Thankfully, she still had a good view of him between her legs.

"Fuck that's sexy," he said as he gazed at her wet slit. He bent in close and inhaled, slowly, as though savoring a good cigar or fine wine. Even when he straightened, he didn't look away. "Pink, wet, needy. You want me to make you feel good, gorgeous?"

Each word that left his mouth only served to ramp up her desire. His potent effect on her wasn't lost on him. He watched as more arousal eased from her body, preparing her for whatever he had in mind. And he needed to get on it soon or she might have to take matters into her own hands, literally. As it was, her nipples had tightened to aching points of need and her pussy craved to be filled by him. Any part of him.

He seemed to be as affected as she was if the shallowing out of his breaths was any indication. As though he sensed her train of thought, he cupped himself, rubbing a hand over his erection through the thick denim.

She licked her lips. With a tortured groan, he dropped to his knees between her spread legs. Being six-foot-two was an advantage in this case, allowing his mouth to line up perfectly with her center.

But still, he waited, watched, breathed.

Alyssa could barely swallow around the thickness in her throat. "Please," she whispered, low and with such desperation. She couldn't remember a time when the need for him was such a harsh demand. As though it was essential to her survival.

"Tell me what you need."

Anything he was willing to give. "I need you to do something. Touch me, lick me…anything."

"Anything?" he practically growled.

"Mmm," was all she could manage.

Without warning, he turned his head and sunk his teeth into the tender skin of her inner thigh, just inches away from the junction connecting her leg to her pelvis.

"Oh my God," she cried, as the sharp sting of his teeth registered. She really wasn't into pain but liked riding that fine line between pleasure and pain, where the sensations morphed together to intensify the ecstasy.

Laving the mark with his warm tongue, he forged a path closer and closer to where she longed for him most. When he reached her empty pussy, he took a long lick straight up to her clit, flicking it with his tongue.

"Oh, thank you," she said on a breathy exhalation as her hips arched to meet his face.

His low chuckle vibrated against her, eliciting a sharp gasp. Then it was as though her taste hit his senses and he lost all control. Unyielding hands gripped her ass and yanked her to the very edge of the counter, eliciting a high-pitched yelp. Then he buried his face in her pussy and she cried out as intense pleasure swamped her entire body.

For the past two years, her world had been spinning on a different axis. Upside down, backward, doing crazy loop-de-loops. All it took was a few seconds of pleasure and connection to someone she loved more than her own life to bring everything to a grinding halt, then get it rotating again in the right direction.

Now, how to get back to the point where this was an everyday occurrence? Because only then would she finally heal and move forward with her life.

With their life.

CHAPTER EIGHT

Everything that didn't involve the feeling of Tyler's mouth on her sex faded into the background. The confusion of her strained marriage, persistent grief over her daughter's passing, the stress of being back to work after so long—it all disappeared for a short while as Tyler reminded her of what it was like to be a desirable woman.

And a ravaged woman.

How had it come to this? Why could they only connect as strangers? How come Alyssa and Derek had to pretend to be other people to find the connection that once came so easy?

He showed her no mercy, sucking on her outer lips with strong pulls, circling her clit with his tongue then drawing it into his mouth, spearing her opening with his agile tongue. Never was he in one spot for too long, and just when she'd get used to a new and intense sensation, he'd switch it up, sending her reeling once again.

"Christ," he mumbled against her pussy. "I thought you smelled amazing, but it's nothing compared to how fucking incredible you taste."

His teeth grazed her clit and she cried out, reaching for his head on instinct. Unfortunately, her carefully balanced position didn't allow her to lift an arm and she toppled down onto the island. With a growl of frustration, she tucked her elbow back against her side and pushed up.

Escapades

What had been the plan anyway? Pull him closer? Push him away? Just hold on and ride out the storm?

It didn't matter. A pleasant tingling sensation started in the tips of her fingers and toes, extending through her limbs. When he shoved his tongue inside her yet again, her pussy clamped down and she threw her head back as flashes of light shot through her vision. "I'm gonna come," she cried out.

"Give it to me." The barked command, combined with the way he wrapped his lips around her clit and sucked hard, threw her over the edge.

"Shit," she yelled, as pleasure crested over her in waves. It had been ages since she had an orgasm like this, one that made the world quake beneath her. One that made her soul sing and left room for nothing in her head but joy. Only one man had ever been able to wring that kind of toe-curling response from her.

After that powerful release, her body tried to come down to a sated state of lethargy, but Tyler had other plans. He didn't let up, didn't ease or gentle in his devouring of her. Had he not noticed the monster orgasm that ripped through her?

No, that wasn't possible.

Her body had been spasming, out of control, and she hadn't stifled her cries.

He was just on a mission to bring her to the edge yet again. The only problem was she was sensitive from the recent orgasm, beyond sensitive, really. And he went at her like a man possessed. Like he was unaware of anything but her pussy and his hunger.

"It's too much," she said with a moan. "I can't take it—oh God, it's too much. You have to stop." She tried again to reach for him, but as before, was thwarted by an inability to hold herself up without her arms.

If she survived this, she'd be hitting the gym every day. Clearly, she was lacking in the abs department.

With a grunt, he left her pussy and stood, drawing a sigh of both relief and frustration from her. The reprieve didn't last more than two seconds. Two thick fingers slid into her, taking the place of his mouth in driving her crazy. With his free hand, he yanked the lacy bra cups down, exposing her neglected breasts and bent to suck one nipple into his mouth. He only spent maybe three seconds on her breast, but the strength with which he drew on it had her moaning. Then he switched to the other breast and treated it to the same brief but intense treatment.

She could barely keep up with the overwhelming riot of sensations when he took her lips in a fierce kiss, infusing her with her own flavor. The kiss was as brief as his attention on her breasts but just as powerful. "You'll take what I give you. Everything I give you. Got it?"

His fingers curled inside her, finding the spot that made her eyes cross and she nodded. Always. She'd give him anything he wanted and take everything he dished out for as long as she lived.

"Say it," he commanded.

"A-anything you want to give me…everything."

"Damn straight." He dropped down to his knees once again and added his mouth back into the mix. While he fucked her with his fingers, he licked and sucked around her clit like it was his favorite treat.

On the barstools, her overtaxed leg muscles quivered and shook with the effort to maintain the position. If she let her legs go, she'd probably slide right off the bar. The muscles in her stomach began to twitch and tremble and her shoulders ached from bracing herself up. She was torn between the desire to flop back on the bar and give her exhausted body a rest or continue watching the erotic sight of Tyler eating her out for all he was worth.

In the end, she couldn't look away, transfixed by the sight of the almost animalistic way he pleasured her. Tears filled her eyes. It had been far too long since she felt this incredible. And not just the physical pleasure, but the connection to another person, the loss of control, and knowledge that she wasn't the only one in so deep.

Wasn't the only one lost to the madness.

His name was on the tip of her tongue and she longed to yell it at the top of her lungs. To make sure he knew she associated the indescribable pleasure with him, but it wasn't the right name. She couldn't bring herself to utter it. Only one man's name would ever cross her lips in the throes of passion and *Tyler* wasn't it. This time, there was no buildup to the orgasm. It slammed into her before she had time to prepare for it. She screamed with the force of release as the room went black.

At some point, while she was coming with the force of a category five hurricane, her upper body failed her. When the world came back into focus, she was staring at the ceiling with her back flat on the island. She twitched and jumped with aftershocks and her skin felt so hypersensitive, she was afraid to do so much as brush against Tyler.

She could only imagine the picture she made. Heels still on, legs spread wide on the barstools, skirt rucked around her waist, open top, bra yanked down, hair a wild mess. Probably pretty damn hot.

With a chuckle, she struggled to a semi-upright position. At least upright enough to see Tyler. "I'm glad to know I'm still alive after that insanity. If you give me two minutes to gather my strength, I'll return the fav—"

Uh-oh.

There was no arrogant male conqueror look on his face. Nor was there the smoky desire that had been present earlier. And he didn't look like a man who was ready to have his own world rocked. He looked more like a man who just received devastating news.

"What's wrong?"

"I...I can't. I'm sorry. I can't do this." He ran a hand through his hair, scattering the short strands. Some of his beard still glistened with the evidence of her arousal.

"Can't do what?" Nerves skittered across her skin, dimming some of the afterglow she should have been basking in. Couldn't be with her? She held her breath waiting for an answer that had the power to destroy her.

"Um…this. Right now. I can't do this." He waved a hand between them and around the room. "I'm sorry, Alyssa. So fucking sorry for all of it."

With that step out of character, he spun and charged for the door.

"Derek, wait!"

The slam of the door echoed through the quiet room making her jolt. She waited for a moment, listening for the sound of his own hotel suite door banging closed, but was greeted with only silence. He must have left the floor.

Alyssa sat up straight and began the task of righting her disastrous clothing. Well, shit. She'd pushed too hard. So hard, he'd abandoned the game and called her Alyssa.

Had it all been one colossal mistake? Sure, the idea had been radical, a Hail Mary attempt to save the most precious thing in her world. Maybe he just needed time. That had to be it.

That *had* to be it.

Because the alternative wasn't acceptable. The notion that he was done with her, didn't want her anymore…

Her stomach rolled, and tears flooded her eyes. She wouldn't go down without a fight. The first devastating loss she experienced nearly did her in. Derek was her world. Until she met him, she'd thought stories of true love and romance were exaggerated tales made for books and movies. But Derek was made for her. There was no other way to describe it. He made her whole and she was confident she did the same for him. She couldn't breathe without him and didn't plan on learning how.

No way in hell would she throw her marriage away without giving it all she had.

CHAPTER NINE

Derek stormed toward the elevators with his heart in his throat, trembling hands, and the intoxicating tang of his wife still lingering on his lips. His cock was harder than it had been in years and his balls ached with the need for release. A raging case of blue balls was the least he deserved for walking out on Alyssa before the sweat had cooled on her soft skin.

When he thought of how long it had been since he'd tasted her, pleasured her like that, seen her give herself over the pleasure she loved, he felt physically ill.

For years, he'd lived for that. Lived for the needy whimpers she made when she wanted him. Lived for her tantalizing contradiction of shy and sensual. Lived for the way she responded to him and only him. Lived for every moment he spent with her.

And now?

Now he felt like he barely knew the woman who should have been his whole world. Had no clue what went on in her days recently. Didn't even know she'd gone back to work. Didn't know if she was sleeping through the night or plagued with worries and grief. How had this happened? How had he let it happen? He'd failed her miserably. So wrapped up in his own grief and selfish inability to deal with his feelings that he'd shut himself off and neglected the rare and priceless connection they shared.

As the elevator reached the ground floor, he pulled out his phone and fired off a text to Brett. *Take you up on the offer of an ear. Meet at Pint's?* It was their favorite neighborhood bar. He needed a drink and didn't need to be drinking alone at this point. Maybe hanging with Brett would help him get his head on straight.

His phone chirped.

Already there, one drink in.

Well, that was convenient. Derek stepped into the frosty evening and headed in the direction of the bar. He bypassed the metro station. A long walk would do him good.

Twenty minutes later, he sat on a stool next to his buddy at the bar. Brett had his favorite beer waiting for him. It was then, he realized, just what a lucky bastard he was. He'd neglected his relationship with his wife, yet she was willing to do anything to salvage what they had. Even try a radical plan that had him staying in a hotel, but turned out to be hot as fuck.

He'd also neglected his friendship with Brett, yet the moment he texted in need of an ear, his buddy was there for him, no questions asked. Two of the most important people in his life suffering from his inability to deal with his feelings and heartache were both willing to fight for him. More willing than he'd been apparently.

What an undeserving ass he was.

"So," Brett said, "you ready to spill about what's going on with you and Lyss?"

No preamble, no small talk. Just dive right into the heart of the problem. Classic Brett. And very much appreciated.

Derek sipped his beer. "No."

Brett grunted. "Okay, listen. You need to talk. Get out of your fucking head. I promise your balls won't shrivel up."

Studying his beer like it held all the answers, Derek sighed. If he talked, opened that floodgate, all the pain he was trying to avoid would come crashing in with the power of Niagara Falls.

"I'm good to sit here all night if we gotta."

Shit. "Fine. I'll talk."

A smile lit Brett's face. "'Bout fuckin' time, brother. Go ahead. Spill your guts. Dr. Brett is here for ya."

A laugh burst out of Derek, easing some of his tension. "Shit, it must be worse than even I realized if I'm using you as my marriage counselor."

"Pfft. I'm damn good with the ladies and you know it."

Derek sipped his beer. "Kick her to the curb and find another isn't exactly the advice I'm looking for."

With a roll of his eyes, Brett flipped him off. "Drink more. You know damn well I wouldn't say that about Alyssa. She's always been my favorite person."

A ghost of a smile curled Derek's lips. Brett may be a notorious womanizer, but he treated them all well. From the moment he'd met Alyssa years ago, he'd had a soft spot for her. And she'd always thought of him as a big brother of sorts.

"Well, as you picked up on, things haven't been right with Alyssa and me since..." The words just wouldn't come out of his mouth.

Brett sat, a patient expression on his face. His friend was there for him for sure, but wasn't going to give him a pass. He'd make Derek say the words.

He cleared his throat. "Things haven't been right since Katie died." There. He'd said it. Given voice to it. And got the stab of pain in his heart was just as sharp as it had been the day it happened.

Brett nodded and let Derek speak. He tempered his voice and tried to keep from being pummeled with emotions he didn't want to feel. As he confided in his friend, Derek's mind replayed the past year, but especially the events of the past week and a half.

Thirteen Days Ago

Derek pushed the door open and smiled at the professional woman with a long, deep brown braid over her shoulder and dark rimmed glasses perched atop her head. Damn, she couldn't be much older than he was. Hell, she may have been younger. For some reason when he imagined the marriage counselor, he pictured an older, sophisticated woman spouting wisdom borne of a long healthy marriage.

With an apologetic smile, he cast a glance at the plush couch where his wife sat, her back straight and hands folded in her lap. Ever the lady. Though a nervous lady if her posture was any indication. She may have been rigid and tapping her foot, but her eyes shone with genuine happiness to see him.

Since he was fifteen minutes late, she probably thought he bailed. "Um, hey, babe, sorry I'm late. My last client was a little woozy after a few hours in the chair."

The therapist checked her watch and motioned toward the couch. "Actually, Mr. Jackson, I was running a bit behind as well, so you're right on time. We haven't even formally introduced ourselves yet. Please, take a seat."

He took the space next to Lyss on the couch and threaded his fingers through hers. They trembled in his hand until she clasped him so tight it nearly hurt. She must be even more nervous than she appeared.

He wanted to reach out to her. To drag her into his arms and promise her everything would work out. But he didn't. It was an unnerving feeling. This uncertainty. This absence of confidence in his relationship. He felt as though he'd forgotten how to touch her.

Not for sex. That he damn well remembered.

But this deeper intimacy. Comforting, reassuring, loving…

Had he really closed himself off that much? So much that he couldn't remember how to touch his wife?

Christ, he was an asshole.

He hadn't exactly been enthused about the idea of counseling when she broached the subject, but he loved his wife, and wasn't enough of an asshole to deny her something that might help her, or them.

Escapades

"I'm Doctor Margret Appwater, but I like to keep this as informal as possible, so please call me Maggie." She smiled at Lyss, and his wife lost some of the starch and tension in her spine.

"Derek and Alyssa, I presume? And is it okay if I use your first names?"

He nodded while Alyssa said, "That's correct. And, please, those names are fine."

Maggie nodded and jotted notes on her pad. "All right, I'm not one for bullshit or much small talk, so I'd like us to just dive right in."

Derek snorted. He had plenty of experience with therapy, though it seemed a lifetime ago. PTSD was a nasty bitch and had had him in her clutches for years after he left the Navy. For the life of him, he couldn't remember any of the therapists using the word bullshit. Maybe this Dr. Appwater wouldn't be so bad after all.

"Given the nature of my practice, I've heard it all. I want you to feel comfortable enough to say anything, and I mean anything. I promise, it is not possible to shock me, and I also promise you will not tell me anything I haven't dealt with before. There will never be any judgment. Okay?"

Alyssa nodded, but Derek had no idea what she was talking about. "I'm sorry, the nature of your practice? You mean marriage counseling?" He glanced at his wife who wouldn't meet his gaze.

Maggie kept her attention on her notepad. "Well, yes and no. I mean the fact that I specialize in couples and individuals with sexual and intimacy issues. So, I'm going to dive right in with my first question, then I'll let you speak freely. When was the last time the two of you engaged in any type of physical intimacy?"

What. The. Fuck.

Alyssa was unsatisfied with their sex life? Since when? He wanted to laugh out loud. There was no way in hell. She loved sex. Loved sex with him. Even after eight years together she responded to him like she was made for him and he could practically make her come by whispering filthy words in her ear. He was pretty damned certain they had the hottest sex life of anyone they knew.

Christ, the thought that he wasn't satisfying his wife had nausea rolling through his gut. No, it just wasn't possible. The last time they'd had sex she came four times, screaming his name and pulling his hair so hard he teased her and bought a box of Rogaine the next day. And that was just...what?

"Two years ago." The words left Alyssa's mouth in a small, sad voice the exact moment his brain registered the timeline.

Two years ago.

Derek's jaw dropped, and he faced his wife. How on earth had he gone two years without her touch, her taste, without watching her face as she came, without hearing the sound of his name escape her lips in a fit of ecstasy?

That really couldn't be possible.

But her dejected smile and his own memory said it was more than possible. It was true.

"Okay, thank you for being honest. I'd like to get a little background on you guys. Let's start with you, Alyssa, since you're the one who initiated the appointment. Derek, I understand you took a little convincing."

He nodded, like an idiot, unable to form words around the shock filling every cell of his being.

Lyss cleared her throat and cast him a sideways glance. "We've been married for seven years, dated for just six months before that. Derek is eight years older than I am. I had a very conservative, I'd say repressed, upbringing. I'd only slept with one man before him." The rapid rambling was cute but showed her discomfort with talking about personal topics. "Derek and I clicked on so many levels, but sexually..." She blew out a breath and fanned herself.

Damn straight it had been hot as hell. And she most certainly had been brought up in a repressed, strict, over-the-top-religious household. The fact that he'd been the man to draw the latent sexuality out of her was a huge source of pride for him.

She'd trusted him enough to give her body over to him and allow him to teach her all about pleasure. That was never something he'd valued or even given any thought to in a partner, but once he'd met Lyss, it all changed.

She'd been timid, modest, almost afraid of the powerful chemistry between them, but damn had she been curious. Underneath he'd sensed a simmering passion she had no idea what to do with. Not that it was a surprise. She'd been raised in what was only a hop, skip, and a jump from being a cult.

Drawing the passion out of her, nurturing that untapped side of her, exploring her every need had been incredible. She'd told him so many times through the years that he was the only man she could have ever trusted enough to explore her deepest fantasies. Feel the freedom to express her desires, which ran deep.

He loved the fact that there wasn't another man on the planet who knew his wife like he did. Knew how to make her purr, knew how to make her scream. Knew that under her reserved, private personality was a wild woman who loved to give and receive pleasure.

After clearing her throat, Lyss continued. "For us, sex has always been an extremely important part of our relationship." A pretty pink flush stole across her cheeks. No matter how down and dirty their sex life got, she'd always had difficulty talking about anything sexual with anyone but him. That contradiction was something he found adorable.

Maggie smiled. "Remember what I said, nothing is off limits. And there isn't anything to feel bashful about. I've literally heard it all."

"We are, um were, pretty adventurous I guess I'd call it." She turned to him and seemed to lose all fear of sharing as she focused solely on him. "I wanted to do anything and everything with Derek. The foundation of our relationship wasn't built just on sex, but it was a high priority for both of us. It was how we communicated, how we connected, even how we fought. We had sex at least once a day, and it was very rare that we let a day go by without it. That didn't even change after Katie was born." Her smile turned down.

The mention of his daughter's name sent a familiar spear of sadness through his chest.

"All of our friends complained about the dip in their sex lives after a child, or during high-stress times in their lives, but not us. We craved each other, like a drug. Passionate sex, playful sex, comforting sex, angry sex." She shrugged. "I loved it all. Any and every way I could get him. Anywhere, anytime." Her blush intensified.

"Sounds like something to be envious of." The therapist stopped taking notes and gave Lyss her full attention.

Derek had been captivated by her as well. She'd been beyond sheltered when they met, and he'd taken great pleasure in corrupting her. With him, she felt free to express herself, ask for what she wanted, hell, take what she wanted. But never had he heard her talk about their sex life to another person. She was tightlipped and shy outside their marriage. Hell, even her best friend Roxie complained that Lyss never gave her any dirty details to live vicariously through.

"It was. And it was the same no matter what happened in our lives. We survived significant disapproval from my family." She paused and gave a small huff.

Somehow, he managed to hold in a snort. Disapproval was the least of what they'd had to overcome from Alyssa's family who were religious to the point of insanity. But that was the past and had nothing to do with their present problems.

"We survived Derek's PTSD, and both of us working crazy hours to grow our businesses. Nothing shook our bond. Whenever we had stress, we turned to each other and conquered every battle as a pair. We were connected on every level."

"And then?" Maggie gentled her voice, prompting his wife, and his stomach clenched.

Then it all when to shit.

"And then Katie got sick."

A strong fist gripped Derek's heart and squeezed with the force of a thousand men. They hadn't talked about any of this. Because of him. Because he was the selfish asshole who couldn't handle talking about the death of their baby girl. The child who brought so much joy to every aspect of their lives.

Tears filled Lyss's sad blue eyes and spilled down her cheeks. Maggie handed her a box of tissues.

"Lyss," he said.

"Derek, we'll get to you in a moment. I want Lyss to have a chance to get this all out, okay?"

"Okay." Who did that ravaged voice belong to? Surely not him.

Lyss sniffed and set the box of tissues next to her on the luxurious couch. "Katie was just over three when she was diagnosed with cancer, and overnight every single aspect of our lives changed. I closed my business and took care of her while Derek was at work. When he was home, he went above and beyond to make sure I took care of myself as well as helping care for our baby." She looked at him, love shining from her eyes.

"We were so consumed with doctors' appointments, money concerns, medical procedures, chemo, the horror of Katie's pain." She shuddered. "Sex just stopped, and for a while I honestly didn't notice." Her voice lowered to a whisper. "It's been over a year since Katie's passing. I think about her every single day. I miss her every single second. But life seems to be moving forward despite our loss. I feel like I'm finally waking up after a two-year-long nightmare, and while nothing will ever completely fill the void in our lives, we have no choice but to continue on."

"Lyss are you concerned that Derek is seeking a sexual relationship from another woman?"

Every muscle in Derek's body tensed and his breath stilled in his lungs.

Never.

Never had he even had one ounce of desire to sleep with another woman after he met her. Christ, if that was Lyss's concern, he might just break down and cry, something he'd only allowed one time in his life. At Katie's bedside when she took her last breath.

"No." Lyss spoke with a firm voice, and leaned in and pressed a quick kiss to his lips. "That is not something I worry about. Derek would never. He'd stay with me and faithful for the next fifty years, even if we never had sex again. I'm one hundred percent certain of that. And that's what concerns me. I'm terrified that this part of who we are that is so important to me, and that I'm coming to crave again, is dead. That we won't be who we were, and we'll never get that back. We're disconnected outside the bedroom as well as inside. Living more like roommates. Not talking about anything important, not eating together, not spending any quality time together, no dates. We've already lost more than anyone should. I'm not sure what I would do if we lost the core of who we are as a couple."

"Thank you for your honesty, Lyss. Derek, I'd like to hear your thoughts on everything your wife has said."

Shit. His thoughts? The only thought he had right then was that he wanted to go home and fuck his wife until neither of them could see straight. To apologize for the pain she'd been experiencing. But he couldn't. Something locked up inside of him the day Katie died. In the year since her passing, he hadn't found the key to release it yet.

Maybe this therapist could change that.

CHAPTER TEN

Alyssa stepped back and surveyed the master bathroom with a keen eye. Yesterday, yellow and gray towels had hung from the bar, a bright yellow canvas with the words *you are my sunshine* had hung from the wall, and all the other décor fit with the yellow and gray color scheme. Today, she'd replaced just about everything, yellow with teal accents. Now a giant print of a gorgeous teal lily hung from the wall.

She was forever changing up the décor in the house. Something would catch her eye. One piece. A vase or decorative bowl and suddenly an entire design plan would be born. Derek teased her about it constantly, saying there was more than one occasion where he thought he'd come home to the wrong house after work because of her changes.

Hazard of being married to an interior decorator.

Derek…

She closed her eyes and pressed her fingertips against her eyelids as flashes of yesterday's confusing encounter with Derek attacked her brain. How could something so perfect have gone so bad so fast?

But it had.

He'd run out leaving her feeling confused and vulnerable. Also aching for the pain he was in. The pain he wasn't sure how to deal with.

She straightened and reached for the medicine cabinet. Time for some ibuprofen. The sleepless night and constant running of her mind had her head throbbing.

While she was in the medicine cabinet, she grabbed an empty pill bottle and tossed it in the trash. She'd finished the antibiotic a week and a half ago and had forgotten to get rid of the bottle. Three weeks ago, while searching for something in her garage in her socked feet, she'd stepped on a nail. It had scraped bottom of her foot, but really, she'd barely even felt it.

That was until she'd woken up to a red and angry scratch the next morning. Her physician wasn't overly concerned since it wasn't deep, but he put her on an antibiotic to ward off an infection.

It cleared right up and within two days she wasn't even aware of it anymore. Easy fix. The only thing the doctor had warned her about was being diligent about using alternate birth control since antibiotics could render her pill ineffective for the cycle.

She'd almost laughed in the doctor's face. Like that was a problem for her. She hadn't had sex in—

"Oh my God," she said on a gasp as she dropped the ibuprofen and stared at herself in the mirror.

How could she be so stupid?

She'd slept with Derek. No condom, of course. Because she was on birth control. Damnit. The timing was right as well.

Her chest tightened and the image in the mirror swam before her eyes.

She could be pregnant.

Pregnant.

This wasn't happening. This was not something she could handle. She wasn't ready. Would she ever be ready again?

Pursing her lips, she got her breathing under control and stared at the freaked-out woman in the mirror. "It's okay. It was one time. And the pill probably worked."

But what if it didn't? She hadn't even thought about more children until Maggie brought it up in their therapy session.

"Don't panic," she told her reflection. "You're not pregnant."

Fourteen Days Ago

A miniscule amount of guilt settled like a stone in the base of Alyssa's stomach. She'd led Derek to believe this was just another grief counseling session, a kind of year-one check in. But it wasn't. It was wild pitch, a crazy idea to save the relationship she felt slipping through her fingers like water.

Something deep inside of her truly believed if they didn't get their sex life back on track, and soon, their relationship would suffer irreparable damage. What she'd researched of Dr. Appwater's methods was…interesting to say the least, and appealed to the side of Lyss that was dying to be fucked by her husband.

So there they were, in the therapist's office and Lyss had just shared more of what had been running through her head than she had in ages.

"Thank you for your honesty, Lyss. Derek, I'd like to hear your thoughts on everything your wife has said." Their therapist turned toward him.

Her handsome and strong husband scrubbed his hand down his bristly face. That beard was getting a little out of control. Unkempt. With his other hand, he gave her a reassuring squeeze.

"I just…I mean…shit, I have no idea how this happened. Like Lyss said, we've always been…active. There's never been a time where I didn't want her. I can't explain how, but I'm completely shocked to hear it's been two years."

"Losing a child, especially to a drawn-out and painful illness, changes you. I would be floored if your relationship didn't suffer to some extent. But it's unhealthy to let those changes rule your life. As your wife said, no matter how you two feel, or what you've endured, life will still move forward. The healthy thing to do is learn how to deal with your emotions so that you can progress forward as well. That's where most couples fail. They become absorbed in their own grief, sadness, and pain, inadvertently neglecting their partner. A relationship can only survive for so long in that state."

Is that what happened here? Was she so lost in her own anguish she'd neglected her husband? It was a sobering thought. One that came with a healthy dose of guilt. Derek was so important to her, so vital to her existence, the idea that she might have emotionally deserted him when he needed her was a difficult pill to swallow.

"I hear you, doc," Derek said. "I just…didn't even seem to notice that two years had gone by and I'm not quite sure how I buried my head so deep in the sand. I—" He shook his head.

What was he going to say? Lyss was dying to know but didn't want to push him to admit something he wasn't ready to voice.

"Please, Derek, continue." Maggie waited, her pen poised over her notepad.

"I, uh, oh fuck it." Derek winced. "Sorry, doc."

Their therapist chuckled. "Please, no need to censor yourself in any way."

"Okay then." He leaned forward and rested his elbows on his knees, his hand still clutching hers. "There isn't anything in this world that I find better than fucking my wife."

Heat rushed to Lyss's face and she wasn't sure it was purely embarrassment. She felt the same way and the idea that they were working to get back there again wasn't lost on her hungry body. Moisture pooled between her thighs as she listened to Derek's intoxicating voice and watched his sinful mouth move as he spoke. Damn, that mouth could do things that should be illegal, and perhaps were in some states.

"I could have her three times a day and it wouldn't be enough. Hell, maybe that's excessive, but it worked for us. We were pretty much insatiable. No surface of our house was safe from us." He chuckled and turned to her.

Her breath sped up at the molten look he gave her. Like a man starving, his intense gaze ate her up. Derek didn't seem to care at all that they were being observed, and Lyss found herself disregarding that fact as well. How long had it been since he'd looked at her like that? Like he could barely restrain himself from throwing her down and tearing her clothes off, witnesses be damned. They both knew the thrill of having sex in public.

With a wink, he broke the connection. "So, doc, how do we get back to where we were? I'm not stupid enough to believe we can just ignore the last two years."

As she spoke, Maggie tapped her pen against the notepad. "You're absolutely right, Derek. You have to acknowledge those years and deal with them to move forward. Before I lay out my plan, I'd like to ask you one more question. Have either of you considered the possibility of having another child?"

Every drop of air in Alyssa's lungs whooshed out in a hurricane force gust. This question entered her consciousness every single day and she shoved it away as though it were an attacker bent on harming her. She inhaled on a sharp wheeze, unable to fully inflate her lungs due to the constriction in her chest.

"Babe, you okay?"

She blinked and concentrated on Derek's concerned face.

"Alyssa, you seem to be having a strong reaction to the question." In her customary patient way, Maggie waited for her to be ready to speak.

"I can't—" She shook her head. "I can't even think of that question. It hurts too bad." Geez, it was like a knife straight to the heart. "The thought of opening myself up to that kind of pain again, the risk of another loss..." Her shoulders rose and fell. "It's too much at this point."

"And you, Derek?"

"Jesus, I just don't know. The end was so...so fucking awful."

Seeing her strong husband at a loss was almost as painful as the question itself.

Maggie nodded. "Not an uncommon reaction, and perhaps a subconscious reason for avoiding intimacy both physical and emotional."

Huh. A bright lightbulb went off in Lyss's head. Sure, she was on the pill, but nothing was a guarantee. Had she been avoiding Derek to avoid the possibility of becoming pregnant? It wasn't a mystery she'd solve in the next few seconds. It would take some soul searching. Something she'd also avoided since Katie's death. Too painful. When had she become such a coward?

One thing she was coming to realize though was that the distance between her and her husband wasn't simple. It was like a complex tangled string wound in a hundred knots. Untying them would take time, effort, and patience, but Maggie seemed qualified to guide them through which one to pick apart first.

"Okay, you two." Maggie's smile was almost sheepish. "I've developed a program that I think will work very well for you guys. It seems to have the most success in couples who are very sexually active. Now I'll warn you. My program is not yet based on any scientific evidence. I'm working on a grant proposal, so I can begin collecting data and gathering evidence to support the treatment protocol. That being said, I've had great success with it in my practice, so I'm hoping you're open to it and will follow the guidelines. I'm certain it will help you over the hump and get you back on your way to connecting as a couple."

Lyss risked a glance at Derek. One of his eyebrows was arched in a skeptical gesture.

Maggie chuckled. "I want you to spend two weeks apart from each other." She held up a hand when Derek's mouth opened. "Let me lay it out then I'll answer all your questions. I promise. Lyss, you stay in the house. Derek, you get a hotel for two weeks. You're both to use this time apart to work on yourselves. Soul searching, career advancement, organize the house, plan nights out with friends. Figure out exactly what you want, what you need, and what you feel is the block to achieving those things. Focus on the parts of life that have all been on hold since

Katie's illness and death, because I guarantee your sex life wasn't the only thing to suffer.

"In these two weeks, you are to have two dates with each other. Derek, you plan a date in the first week. Dinner, drinks, movie, whatever you want. Two rules for the date. One, the night must end in sex. And, two, you are not Derek or Alyssa for the night. Make up names, make up life stories, have some fun with it."

She turned to Lyss. "You aren't a grieving mother and Derek, you aren't a grieving father. Put it away for one night and connect as two people. Two strangers, or two coworkers, or two individuals who met online. However you want to play it. I want you to connect with each other without the baggage of the past two years. Have fun with it. You can't do that as Derek and Alyssa right now. But, let's say, Kyle and Jenny? Well they can burn up the sheets without anything hanging over their heads. With me so far?"

Lyss nodded, her head swirling with a million runaway thoughts. Was this idea nuts? Would her husband go for it? Would it help them recapture the closeness they'd shared for years? Beside her, Derek looked just as bewildered, but if she wasn't mistaken, quite intrigued and maybe even a little aroused by the idea.

"Lyss, in the second week, you are in charge, but I don't want it to be a formal date. It's a chance meeting. Bump into him on the subway, at the gym, on the street, doesn't matter. But same rules apply. The encounter ends in sex and you are not yourselves. No contact with each other outside of the two dates, unless of course, there is some kind of emergency. We'll meet again after the two weeks are up. What do you think?"

What did she think? She thought it was different. She thought it was crazy. She thought it was…hot.

CHAPTER ELEVEN

The pounding on the door clunked around Derek's head like a lead ball. Shit! Where the hell was he, and how much had he drunk last night? Must have been a helluva lot because only one thing could create this kind of fuzzy-tongued, hammering head —he popped his eyes open and winced—and light sensitivity. And that was a whopper of a hangover.

"Hey, man!" Brett's voice accompanied the continued knocking. "Sorry to wake you, but you've gotta get moving. You have a client in an hour."

Derek blinked a few times until he could tolerate keeping his eyes open for more than two seconds at time. "Thanks. Be out in a minute." Ugh, he sounded as though he swallowed a cup of sand.

Laughter came through the closed door. "You sound pretty rough, D. Coffee's ready. I assume you'll need a vat of it."

With a grunt of agreement, Derek swung his legs over the side of Brett's guest bed, and used the momentum to help haul himself to a sitting position. Coffee would be good. Maybe with a side of Red Bull. Caffeine would be essential to making it through the day.

He pushed to his feet and shuffled toward the door. When he opened it, he was greeted by Brett in his running gear, wearing a sunny smile and a sheen of sweat. "Shit, man, you've been out running already? You're making me look bad."

"I'm the only one here to see, so it ain't a thing. Besides, you needed to get a good drunk on. Helped loosen your lips. Coffee's this way." Brett nudged Derek toward the kitchen.

"Did it ever. Sorry for being such a pussy and puking my emotions all over you."

The teasing light went out of Brett's eyes as he pointed toward a chair and filled a coffee cup. "Shut up, D. That's been a long time coming. You needed to unload more than anyone I've ever met. If it took a bottle of Jack to do it, who cares? I'm just sorry you and Alyssa are going through such a rough patch. Although I like the way this therapist's mind works. What did you say her name was again?"

As the first hit of caffeine slid down Derek's esophagus and into his stomach, he let out a sigh. Wouldn't be long until it hit his bloodstream and hopefully cleared some of the booze-induced fog surrounding him. "No way am I telling you her name. At least not until things are fixed with Lyss. Last thing I need is you pulling a one-and-done on her. Next thing I know she'll be telling Lyss to leave my ass."

"Come on, man. If she can come up with kinky ideas to help her patients, just imagine what she can dream up for herself. I know I'm sure imagining it. Did you tell me what she looked like?"

After draining the last of his coffee, Derek stood. "No, I did not. And I don't plan to. You'll just have to do some more imagining."

"Huh," Brett said. "So if this doc has such a great plan to help you and Lyss get all freaky again, how come you needed to douse yourself in booze last night? I tried asking, but you were too sloppy by that time to talk anymore."

"I do not get sloppy."

Brett laughed. "Man, you were as sloppy as a sorority girl on spring break."

It was impossible for Brett to stay serious for too long. It was also impossible to hate him for it because he was pretty damn funny most of the time. "Fuck you, man," Derek said, then rolled his shoulders. Tension was back now that he was sober. "Lyss and I had our second *encounter* yesterday."

"Oh yeah?" Brett smirked and rubbed his hands together. "Finally, we get to the good stuff. Let me have it. Make my ears bleed with the nasty deets."

"That ain't happening, bro." Derek gulped his coffee and willed the caffeine to work its way through his bloodstream. Sure, in the past he'd shared details of his sex life with Brett, but a lot less once he got together with Lyss. And no way in hell was he going to tell Brett how it felt to bury his face in his wife's sweet pussy for the first time in two years. He would not be sharing how un-fucking-believable it was when she came all over his tongue…twice. Shit, he needed to stop thinking about it or he'd be back in blue-ball purgatory.

"Oh, come on, man. I carted your drunk ass back here and blew off some pretty young thing. You owe me something sexy to make up for it."

Derek inhaled the coffee meant for his stomach and coughed until his eyes watered. "Jesus. I'm not touching that one. In fact, this conversation is over. I'm out."

One hand held up in surrender, Brett pounded Derek's back with the other. "Okay, I'm done busting your balls. Tell me what you wanted to say."

The tone of the discussion changed in an instant. All the feelings he'd tried to drown in a bottle last night came rushing back. He opened his mouth and suddenly found it difficult to put words to his heavy thoughts. "Shit." He ran a hand down his face. "It hit me while I was with her yesterday, just how much I failed her. Two years, Brett. Two fucking years we've been walking away from each other. How did that happen on my watch? That woman…she's fucking everything, and I just let it all fall away."

"Der, this is not a typical situation. It's not like you got in a fight and walked out. You guys went through a serious fucking tragedy."

Derek nodded and scratched through the hair on his chin. "I know. But still, I neglected my marriage. I should have wrapped her up tight and kept her close. Not let her shed a single tear without me being there to wipe it away. But what did I do? Fuckin' haven't touched her in two years. Let's say we fix this. What's to keep me from checking out the next time life gets rough? Maybe she'd be better off—"

"Don't say it. Don't fucking say it, man. It's not true and we both know you don't mean it. You'll hate yourself later if you say it."

That may be true, but he couldn't keep himself from thinking it. Maybe Alyssa would be better off if he let her go. Shit, the pain that came with the thought of leaving her nearly brought him to his knees. But just because it was a pain worse than the bullet he'd taken in Afghanistan years ago, didn't mean it wasn't the right thing for her.

"Look," Brett said as he clapped Derek on the shoulder. "Your head is fucked right now. You won't hear anything I say because you need to take a step back. Don't make any decisions right now. Wait until you see this therapist and hash it out with her and Lyss."

Brett was right. His head was a swirling mess of screwed up emotions. Very masculine. "Yeah. You're right."

"Want something to eat?"

"Nah, I gotta get moving. I'll just grab something from Farad's store. You try those new donuts he's been selling. They're the shit. If I jet now, I'll have just enough time to pick up a few. Mrs. Cromwell doesn't like to be kept waiting."

"I have had the donuts. They're the shit. And Cromwell's your client?" Laughter boomed from Brett. "You're kidding, right? What, another grandchild?"

Mrs. Cromwell was a seventy-eight-year-old woman who got her first tattoo when she was in her fifties. And what a tattoo it was. A full back piece of a giant oak tree. Each time one of her six children blessed her with a grandchild, she added a branch with their names. There were so many branches on the damn thing he wasn't sure how much more of her progeny her back could handle. "First great-grandchild."

"You're shittin' me."

"I kid you not."

"Well." Brett used the hem of his shirt to mop sweat from his forehead, giving Derek a full-on view of his cut abs. "That old bird is something else. Not to mention she makes the best cookies. Sure hope she'll be bringing some by today."

Shit, Brett was still as ripped as they'd been when they were in the Navy. Derek had been as well, until—no surprise there—two years ago. Another thing he'd let fall by the wayside as he failed to conquer his grief and continue on with a life his daughter would have been proud of. Not that he'd let himself get overweight or soft, but he certainly wasn't in top physical shape as he'd once been, and all of a sudden, he realized how much he missed working out. It would probably do him good on a psychological level as well. Time to clear his mind, expend pent-up energy and stress. Though he'd much rather burn it up between the sheets with his wife.

"All right, man. I'm out. I have just enough time to swing by the hotel, shower, and change. I'll see you at the shop. Thanks for letting me crash. And the ear."

Brett lifted his coffee cup in acknowledgement. "No prob. You can pay me back with the good doc's name and digits. See ya later."

With a roll of his eyes, eyes that now felt a bit less bleary, he retrieved his wallet and left Brett's condo, making his way toward the DuPont Circle metro station.

As it turned out, Mrs. Cromwell brought a double batch of cookies to the shop, earning hugs and praise from the staff. She fussed and clucked over everyone like they were her own chicks. As usual her natural maternal instincts endeared her to everyone more than the gift of sugar ever could.

The day flew quickly, which was both good and bad. Good because with each passing hour his hangover lifted a bit more. And bad because each minute that ticked by was one minute closer to his appointment with Lyss and Dr. Appwater and his head was no clearer than it had been early in the day.

If the pit in his stomach was any indication, things with his wife were about to get worse before they got better. If they ever did get better.

CHAPTER TWELVE

This time, Alyssa was the one running late. And she hated to be late about as much as she hated spiders. So, a whole lot. But she'd been so nervous, she spent the first fifteen minutes she should have been driving to the therapist's office hovering over the toilet certain her breakfast was going to reappear. Miraculously it stayed down, but she was now a good few minutes tardy for her appointment despite the fact she blew two red lights. That tidbit would not be shared with Derek. He constantly worried about her safety and tended to flip out if she did anything risky.

The nerves stemmed from the unsettled way their previous encounter ended. For the life of her, she couldn't figure out why Derek left the way he had. And she'd spent far too many hours dissecting every second that they were together. Reliving it again and again had the dual effect of arousing her and making her angry. How could he just storm out like that, leaving her so confused?

She was bound to find out in the next few minutes.

"I'm so sorry I'm late," she called out as she threw open the door to Dr. Appwater's small waiting room.

The pretty young receptionist greeted Alyssa with a smile. "Please don't worry about it, Mrs. Jackson. Maggie is running a few minutes behind herself."

Relief left her in a whoosh of air. "Oh good." She turned to find a chair to wait and froze at the sight of her husband sitting there. "Oh! Derek, hi." Tension stiffened her spine. There wasn't anything worse than feeling awkward around the one person she'd always been able to be her genuine self with. He knew everything about her: good, bad and ugly. Never had he made her feel anything less than beautiful, cherished, and desired, even at her worst. And now there was a divide between them and she had no idea how to bridge the gap.

Should she go sit next to him? Should she give him space?

The uncertainty in what used to be stable and safe sucked.

"Hey, Lyss." He patted the seat next to him and she hesitated a second before closing the distance to him. His posture was stiff and unwelcoming, but a small smile played across his lips. That was a good sign.

Right?

They sat in strained silence for about three minutes, then Maggie opened her door and waved them in. Ever the gentleman, Derek waited for her to precede him. But he didn't take her hand, didn't rest his on the small of her back, didn't touch her at all. And when she sat in the same spot on Maggie's plush couch as she has last time, Derek sat too, but he left a foot of space between them. Twelve little inches that might as well have been a mile-wide chasm.

Maggie must have picked up on the stiffness in the room because she raised one eyebrow as she took her own seat across from them. But if she did sense something was off, she kept it to herself for the time being. "Hey, you two. I'm so sorry to keep you waiting. Thank you for your patience."

"No problem," Derek said.

Alyssa was glad he'd responded. Her insides were coiled so tight and her throat felt so thick, she was afraid she'd start crying if she tried to talk.

The faint smell of grapefruit tinged the air. Perched on a windowsill across the room, a diffuser pumped fragrant steam into the air. Probably essential oils. Grapefruit was great for banishing mental exhaustion and calming anxiety. As an interior designer, Alyssa found clients loved if she went above and beyond recommending personalized touches such as essential oils they might benefit from. She made a point of gifting each client a diffuser and a few oils.

With the way her nerves were on edge, she'd have to bathe in a tub full of grapefruit oil to feel any kind of relief.

"So," Maggie said. "Let's get right into it. Before we speak about your dates, I'd like to know if you each spent some time soul searching? Really thinking and allowing yourself to process your feelings. Alyssa, let's start with you."

"I cleaned out Katie's room," she blurted. Heat rushed to her face. That was totally not an answer to the question Maggie asked, but it had led to some deep introspection, so she supposed it was a good place to start.

"Okay." Maggie jotted some notes on her pad then gave Alyssa her full attention. Today she wore a cream-colored cashmere sweater and simple black slacks. Her glasses rested on her head again. "Tell me about that."

She risked a glance at Derek who was staring at her with a flat, unreadable expression. His handsome face was so closed off and it scared her to death. "Well, I just felt it was time. And I felt like it was what I need to do to shock myself back into the present. My best friend, Roxie, helped me. We got drunk, shared stories about Katie, laughed, and cried. It was actually very cathartic."

She peeked at Derek again. Would he be upset she'd done it without him?

"It's also very healthy, Alyssa. Hanging on to a few memorable keepsakes is perfectly acceptable. No one wants you to try to purge the memory of your daughter, but many parents in your situation keep their child's room for years, decades even, as a sort of shrine to their lost child. They think it will help, but all it does is anchor them to the past. I'm really proud of you for taking that step." She turned her attention to Derek. "What are your thoughts on that, Derek?"

Alyssa held her breath. Her heart was pounding so loud she might miss what he was about to say. "I'm sorry," she announced before he had a chance to speak. "I didn't wait for you. But I thought if we did it together, it would be even harder. Wait, that didn't come out right."

Maggie held up a hand. "It's all right Alyssa, but hold on until Derek speaks. I'd like to hear what he has to say."

He cleared his throat. "She's right. It would have been a clusterfuck if we tried to do it together. Too much grief in one room." His face was still impassive, but he couldn't hide the pain in his voice. "I'm glad it helped you. And that Rox was there for you," he said, turning to Alyssa.

"Thank you," she whispered. Relief hit her so hard, she felt boneless and tired. Like she could lie back on Maggie's couch and sleep for a week. It had been two years since she'd slept through the night. First it was stress and worry over Katie's health, money concerns, work concerns. Then it was grief so strong she'd wake up alone in the middle of the night to a tear-soaked pillow. Every time, she'd tiptoed out of the room in search of Derek, only to find him sitting in front of an infomercial with a blank stare. Not once had she gone to him. She hadn't been able to handle their combined heartache. She was just too weak. Now it was fears of a failed marriage that kept her awake well into the early morning hours. Maybe if she hadn't been so selfish. If she'd gone to him and tried to comfort him they wouldn't be in this position today.

She took a deep breath. It was time. Time to reveal what she'd learned about herself these past two weeks through many hours of introspection, journaling, and reality facing. "One of the things that attracted me to Derek from the first moment I met him…" she started, looking at Maggie.

With a quick shake of her head, Maggie pointed to Derek. "Speak to him, Alyssa, not me."

She nodded and clenched her hands in her lap as she faced the man who owned her heart. "One of the things I fell hard for and still love about you, is your strength."

He gave her a half smile and flexed a colorful bicep that still had the power to make her sex clench, even after all these years. She could have kissed him for trying to lighten the serious mood in the office.

"Yes," she said as her face heated. "But also, your inner strength. You take command and control without being overbearing. You work hard to protect me from anything you think will harm me. You stood up to my family years ago and saved me from a life I didn't want to live. You've overcome your own personal hell. You face every challenge we've ever encountered as though it's no more than an annoying gnat buzzing around. Nothing bests you."

Derek sat quietly and listened to her. She stared straight into his eyes while she spoke and almost forgot Maggie was there as her surroundings faded into background. Everything in her was focused on him.

"But there are still some things that can cut through the strongest steel. What happened to Katie did something to me, inside of me, that I'm not sure I'll ever fully recover from. And I know it did the same thing to you. And I couldn't handle it. I couldn't handle seeing your devastation, your pain."

She dropped her face into her hands as shame swamped her and tears flooded her eyes. "I'm sorry. It's so selfish of me. I'm supposed to be there for you and I just…ch-checked out."

The tears fell in torrents as horrible choking sobs wracked her body. Admitting it out loud, hearing the words, telling Derek that she'd been too lost in her own grief to tolerate his made her feel like the worst wife on the planet.

Derek had tolerated so much because of her, because of her family. He'd been amazing through Katie's illness and she'd abandoned him in his time of need in favor of her own needs.

It was a wonder he could even stand to look at her.

* * *

I couldn't handle seeing your devastation, your pain.

Alyssa's words cut into him, piercing the hard shell he'd erected since Katie's passing. She shouldn't have had to see his devastation. He should have shielded her from it. Protected her from it. Alyssa had needed him strong to guide her through the tragedy.

He'd failed her.

And now they were sitting in a therapist's office trying to glue the broken pieces of their marriage.

His wife wept into her hands. The sounds of her anguish filled the small therapist's office. He should go to her, do something to ease her suffering, but as had become his new norm, he did nothing.

All the emotions he'd been putting in little boxes and shoving into the corners of his mind reached out and wrapped their hands around his neck, choking him for all they were worth. Katie's suffering, his wife's torment, his own loss and feelings of failure. Maggie had asked them for some introspection during their time apart, and even that he'd chickened out on until the previous night. Now, hearing Alyssa's misguided guilt and shame, everything he'd tried to tamp down exploded within him.

It was paralyzing in its intensity. So much so that he couldn't even offer his wife comfort. He was failing her yet again.

"Derek, you look a little green around the gills," Maggie said. "I'd like to get your feelings on what Alyssa just said, but first I'd like to address it myself. Here, Alyssa." She held out a box of tissues. Not the same box as last time. With a practice like hers, she must go through the damn things faster than a whore went through condoms.

"Thanks," Lyss said as she sniffed. "I'm sorry I lost it like that."

"Please don't be," Maggie replied. "I want you to know, Alyssa, that what you're feeling is extremely normal. The tragedy you and Derek experienced is pretty much the worst thing a couple can go through. It's not selfish to have a difficult time seeing your big, strong, SEAL husband crippled with grief."

Derek flinched at her description, but couldn't deny it.

"It's normal," Maggie continued. "It's expected. You love him. You just witnessed someone you love succumb to a horrible disease. It's only natural that you wouldn't want to see anyone else you love suffer. All couples lose their way for a time. Why do you think the divorce rate is so high for marriages in which a child passes? Some people can't stand the sight of their loved one anymore, because it reminds them of their child. Some turn to drugs or alcohol. Some internalize their feelings until they self-destruct. Others withdraw and slowly pull away. But not all couples care enough to find their way back to each other. And you two do. Tell me what you're thinking, Derek."

"Huh? What?" All he could see were Alyssa's red-rimmed eyes and tear-drenched cheeks. All he could hear was the loud voice in his head berating him for neglecting his wife, for failing her, for failing their child. Alyssa deserved a man who would could be there for her. A man who wouldn't pull away from her when the road got rough.

"Derek? You okay?" Lyss asked.

He blinked and looked at the two women gawking at him. One with concern on her beautiful but sad face, and the other with patient understanding. Like she could see into his head and knew he was all sorts of fucked up in that moment, but she wasn't fazed by it.

"I'm sorry," he said. Suddenly the four walls of the office seemed to be closing in on him. He pulled at the neck of his T-shirt to ease the sensation of the fabric tightening. Hell, his own skin felt itchy and too tight like he he it was trying to suffocate him.

He stood. A crushing pressure in his chest made breathing difficult. "I'm sorry. I just...I can't."

"What? Derek—" Alyssa's eyes widened, and she turned as he rounded the couch and sped toward the door.

"Derek, it's all right. Sit back down. I'll get you some water, and we can discuss it," Maggie said.

He reached for the doorknob and shook his head. The heaviness in his chest was almost crushing at that point. Casting one last glance at his wife, he somehow managed to inhale enough air to speak. "I'm sorry."

"Der—"

He didn't wait to hear Alyssa's pleas. He tromped through the door, past a startled receptionist, and out into the chilly November air. Only when he was seated in his SUV could he finally breathe again. And he did just that. Resting his head against the steering wheel and focusing on each steady inhalation.

Shit, he hadn't had a panic attack in years. Not since the early days of his and Lyss's relationship. But he couldn't stand the thoughts running through his head. The bombardment of negative emotions. The insight he'd been lacking over the past year.

And if the weight of guilt over his distressed marriage hadn't been enough to trigger an episode, the shattered look on his wife's face as he fled the office like a chicken shit was.

And the knowledge that there was no one to blame for her devastation but himself only made it worse.

Now she was probably in there crying her eyes out to the therapist when he should be the one to comfort her. Another failure.

He should man up and head back in there, but he couldn't. Not until he had his head on straight.

Shit. Could he have fucked the situation up any worse?

CHAPTER THIRTEEN

Familiar sensations hit him from all angles. The harsh clank of weighted metal plates banging together. The whirring and heavy clop of feet pounding on a treadmill belt. Men and women wiping perspiration from their brows. The subtle stench of sweat that never seemed to vacate the air in the gym.

Muscles he hadn't used in far too long twitched as though anticipating the abuse they were about to take. But instead of dreading it, both he and his muscles were chomping at the bit to get a good workout in. For a SEAL, grueling physical activity was the norm. A part of everyday life. Running, pushups, pull ups, obstacle courses, swimming, martial arts. You name it, his team did it. Every single day. Along with guns, knives, bombs, and basically every weapon the military utilized, their bodies were just as deadly a weapon.

At first, their bodies struggled under the huge physical strain required of them. Hell Week during BUDS training couldn't have been more aptly named. But as time went on, he and his teammates became so accustomed to placing high demands on their bodies, they almost came to crave the intense physical workouts.

Even after leaving the Navy, he'd worked out religiously. In the gym, running on trails, sparring with Brett, shooting at a local range. They hadn't kept to the level of the SEALS, but no one could accuse either of them of being slouches.

Until now, anyway. Well, until almost two years ago when Katie's treatment and care became so time consuming, he gave it up.

With a snort, he made his way to an unoccupied treadmill. That wasn't entirely true. In fact, it was a cop-out. They would have found a way to make it work. Alyssa would have been more than willing to pick up the slack and stay with Katie while he exercised. Hell, Roxie or Brett would have as well.

His inability to deal with the helplessness and failure of every bomb they threw at Katie's illness had him drawing away from it as he'd drawn away from Lyss and everything else in his life. Looking at it now, from a bit of distance, he could really see how he should have kept up with the workouts. Tiring himself out would have helped him sleep. Taxing his muscles to fatigue would have given him an outlet for all the negativity and stress in his life at the time. The quiet time afforded by miles of running would have given him time to process his thoughts and emotions in a more constructive manner than shoving them into a box in his mind.

Hindsight.

The clear-eyed motherfucker.

He stepped on the revolving tread, stuck his earbuds in his ears, and moved through some basic stretches before firing up the machine. Ten minutes into a steady jog, sweat ran down his face in rivers, his heart pounded like the drum solo to *Wipe Out*, and his leg muscles screamed in agony.

Shit, he was in worse shape than he'd assumed.

Pathetic.

After another five minutes, he started to find his groove. Sure, he'd still be left in the dust if he was stupid enough to try to race Brett, but instead of feeling like he was dying, he was enjoying the push-pull of his muscles as he ran.

"Excuse me! Hey, dude, can you hear me?" a woman to his left asked.

Without slowing his pace, he paused the music and yanked an earbud out. A woman in barely-there running shorts and a tight-fitting tank stood in the center of the treadmill to next to his. She was cute, with black hair in a high ponytail, colorful hibiscus tattoos running from her right elbow to shoulder, and hoops through her eyebrow and nose.

"Were you talking to me?" he asked.

"Yeah, sorry to bother you. Just wanted to tell you your ink rocks. Some of the best work I've seen." The girl, probably in her early twenties, pointed to his left arm.

He had a full sleeve, most of it done since he left the Navy, with various tribal tattoos, a few nods to his SEAL brothers, both fallen and living, but the one she stared at was on his forearm. A baby's footprint with angel wings and spanning the entire length and width of his large forearm.

The footprint was copied directly from Katie's baby print, stamped just minutes after birth. He'd done the ink work himself, no easy feat, but it was too personal for another artist. Katie, as many little girls, was obsessed with all things pink and purple, so he'd done the foot in vibrant swirls of those colors. The wings were golden. He didn't give a shit that it wasn't the most masculine of tattoos out there. It was bright, colorful, and cheerful, exactly how Katie should be remembered.

"Thanks," he said as he lifted the earbud back to his ear.

"Where'd you get it done?"

He sighed. Where was she going with this? If she wanted to talk ink, he'd give her a few minutes of his time, but if she was looking for something more than that, she was out of luck. He could appreciate a pretty face, as he was sure Lyss could appreciate an attractive man, but that was as far as it went. In all the years he and Lyss had been together, he hadn't felt so much as a flicker of interest in another woman. Even innocent flirting was a waste of his time and he never engaged in it.

"Place in Adams Morgan. Enjoy your run." There. A dismissal without being an asshole.

The girl chuckled. "I can take a hint. But, dude, I get it. You're married. I can clearly see the wedding ring you keep flashing my way while pretending you're not doing it on purpose." She laughed again then hit some buttons on her treadmill and started a fast walk. "Promise I'm not interested in anything more than some ink talk. You're not *that* good looking." She raised an eyebrow at him. "Ego, much?"

Good thing it took a fuck of a lot to embarrass him, because he'd be mortified if it didn't. And she'd whacked that nail right on the head. He'd been not so discretely angling his left hand so she had a clear view of his wedding ring. He chuckled. Did kind of make him seem like an egotistical bastard.

"Ah, sorry about that. And I did the ink myself." He held up his arm, with Katie's tat facing toward the girl. "That one, anyway."

She whistled. "Damn, now I'm even more impressed. You've got some serious talent. Name's Thea by the way."

"Thanks. I'm Derek. And that's some pretty impressive work you've had done as well."

She smiled and peeked at her shoulder. "Wait—you said a shop in Adam's Morgan? Wouldn't happen to be Trident Ink, would it?"

What the hell? His shop was well known in the area, but they hadn't done her tattoo. He'd have remembered it for sure. It was some damn fine work. The flowers almost looked three dimensional, like they were lifting right off her skin. "That's the one. I own it. Heard of us, huh? We didn't do that shoulder."

"Nah. Had this done in Texas, where I'm from. Just moved here actually and in a strange twist of fate, I have an interview tomorrow at your shop for the piercer position."

Derek's eyes widened. "No shit?" Brett was going to love her, maybe too much.

"No shit," she responded.

"Pretty damn small world, huh? Hope you're not nervous. It will be pretty laid back. I'm assuming you've spoken to Brett? He's my business partner and the other piercer."

She nodded then increased the speed on the treadmill until she was running at nearly his pace. Geeze, he had at least eight inches on her and she had no problem keeping time with him.

Pathetic.

"Yeah, he seems great. He said he'd be the one conducting the interview."

"He will." Derek considered her for a second. She was young, probably not very experienced, but friendly and probably great with customers. Sometimes personality trumped experience, not skill necessarily, but just because she was inexperienced didn't mean she wouldn't be skilled at the job.

He liked her. She'd be a great addition to the shop. "Hey, I'll give you a tip to get on Brett's good side right off the bat. There's a quick mart down the block from the shop, owned by a great guy named Farhad. Drop my name, let him know you need a large of Brett's favorite. He'll hook you up and you'll have Brett wrapped around your finger in no time."

Her face lit up with a radiant smile. She'd obviously understood she had the boss's seal of approval. "Thanks. I'll do that." She started to replace her headphones then turned toward him again. "Wait, what's his favorite?"

Derek snickered. "Mocha latte, heavy on the syrup and extra whip."

A startled laugh bubbled out of Thea. "You're kidding me? Not the most macho of drinks. Brett told me you were both former SEALS."

"Yep. He claims that's why he drinks it. Too many mornings drinking shitty black coffee in the desert. Likes to indulge."

"Well, can't fault him for that. Well, I'll let you get to it. The longer I talk, the more chance I have of saying something stupid and completely ruining my chances of getting the job even before the interview."

He laughed. "I'm sure you'll be fine, but I should focus. I need to at least pretend you wouldn't kick my ass in a race."

She smiled and shoved her earbuds in her ears. "Good talking to you. See you tomorrow." Her ponytail bobbed in time with her steps and she was starting to huff and puff.

Thank God. He could hang on to his man card for another day.

Derek ticked his speed up a few notches and increased his stride. No sense in exercising if he wasn't going to push himself.

The friendly Thea would be a nice addition to their team. Hopefully Brett could resist the temptation to come on to her. They really needed a second piercer and did not need a sexual harassment suit. Not that women ever complained when Brett turned his attention toward them, but there was a first time for everything.

Piercing had become an integral part of their business. Much more than he'd ever anticipated. When they opened shop, Brett barely had enough to keep him busy. But now? Well now they had a waiting list the length of his arm. Hence the interview.

Excitement bubbled under his skin. The shop he'd worked so hard to grow and nurture had made quite a name for itself. And it was continuing to expand. His dream had really come true.

He couldn't wait to tell Lyss. Both about the potential for increased business as well as about the interviewee herself. For some reason, he had a feeling the two would hit it off.

Huh.

That was the first time in a while he'd been excited to share some news with Lyss.

Really it was the first time he'd felt a spark of life about anything. He'd gone through the motions at work, like everything else in his life, but he'd feared he'd lost his passion for it. But now, he felt it again. Enthusiasm. Pride in his business. The desire to work hard and see the results of his efforts.

He smiled and increased his pace yet again.

He was starting to feel human again. And all it took was twenty-five minutes of sweat and fatigue.

Well, that and a few sweaty hours with his wife.

CHAPTER FOURTEEN

"Thanks for staying late, Hannah," Alyssa said to her assistant as she closed her laptop lid. "I can't believe how many clients we've gotten since I came back. I'm swamped. At this rate, I'm going to need to hire another designer before the end of the year."

Tall, with legs for miles and sleek auburn hair that kissed her shoulders, Hannah inclined her head and smirked.

"What?" Lyss asked. "You're dying to say something. I can see it, so spit it out."

Hannah laughed. "You don't see it. That's the thing. You've never seen it."

"Huh? Never seen what?"

"How freakin' talented you are at what you do. And how in demand you were before you closed up shop. Girl, there are people who have been waiting on you to come back for almost two years. People who put their own plans on hold to wait you out. Your designs were in high demand back then and people are ecstatic that you're back in action."

Her jaw dropped. "Clients waited this whole time? You're kidding."

"Nope," Hannah said, curling in her lips so the P popped out. "Not kidding at all. And yes, I've had no less than five phone calls from people who've wanted to remodel their homes and held off because they wanted the best designer. People who live in Potomac no less, so...cha-ching."

Pride filled her. "Wow. Well, if this isn't just a fluke, maybe I should look into adding another designer. I'd hate to have to turn business away because it's more than I can handle myself."

Hannah crossed her long legs and nodded. "I'll get working on a help wanted ad. As soon as it's done, I'll run it by you." Her five-foot-ten-inch assistant-turned-friend wore three inch heels every day.

Alyssa love it. Of course, that meant she got a crick in her neck looking at her, but she was used to staring up at a giant of a man, so...

Ugh. Thoughts of Derek threatened to destroy the I'm-not-a-total-mess mask she'd donned early that morning and managed to keep in place throughout the day. She couldn't obsess over what could be going through her husband's mind and focus on work at the same time.

"Remember how it was in the beginning?" Hannah asked.

Thank God for that distraction to pull her out of thoughts that just might have her blubbering all over her desk.

The memories Hannah brought up had her smiling. "Sure do. I literally built this company with a baby on my hip. We had some seriously understanding clients back in those days." Slowly but surely, she was beginning to think of the wonderful memories she had of her daughter. She'd never get over Katie's death. How could a mother ever get over something so crushing? But the happy memories were accompanied by a tinge of sadness now as opposed to the suffocating despair that came whenever she'd thought of Katie at first.

"Aw," said Hannah, who'd been with her from the beginning. She kicked off her heels and rotated her ankles with a small sigh as she leaned back against one of the oversized chairs in Alyssa's office. "I think clients liked it. Especially female clients. They loved that having a child didn't keep you from pursuing your dreams and that pursuing those dreams didn't keep you from being an amazing mother. Not one person complained when you showed up to a job site or for a consultation with Katie strapped to your chest."

Man, she missed her baby with everything she had. Alyssa's eyes prickled with impending tears remembering those early days. "Thanks, Hannah. That means a lot to me."

Those were some good memories. She'd worked her tail off building her business. Supportive wasn't strong enough a word to describe Derek. He'd encouraged her every step of the way. More than once, she'd been ready to throw in the towel, convinced she just wasn't cut out to be an entrepreneur. Especially as a new mom who was so torn between dual dreams: spending as much time as possible with Katie, and developing a thriving business. But he'd dried her tears, rubbed her tired feet, and reminded her that beneath her exhausted exterior lay a badass fighting spirit, as he'd put it.

So, she'd strapped on a pair of *lady balls*, one of Roxie's favorite expressions, and found a way to make it all work.

Hannah shot her a sympathetic smile. She knew how difficult it was for Alyssa to speak about anything Katie related. At thirty, Hannah was still single and claimed she'd be that way forever for some unknown reason. She was quite vocal about not needing a man in her life. But Alyssa never bought it and was convinced Hannah would fall and fall hard one day. Regardless, she was one of the sweetest and most compassionate people Alyssa had ever met. Not to mention one of the most organized and hard working.

She glanced at her watch. "Geez, I didn't realize it was so late. Go on and get out of here. You can work on the ad on Monday."

"And what about you? You getting ready to leave?" Hannah asked as she rose and slipped back into her nude pumps.

"You bet. I'm five minutes behind you." That was a lie. She planned on working until her eyelids drooped and she was so tired she'd be guaranteed to sleep. Otherwise, she'd just lie in her empty bed and fixate on everything that happened at the therapy appointment. Just as she'd done the prior night.

"Okay. I'll see you Monday." Hannah strode out of the office with all the confidence of someone who knew they looked good. And she did. Always.

"Close the door behind you if you don't mind," Alyssa called out. "And have a good weekend."

When the door clicked shut, she leaned back in her chair and rolled her neck along her shoulders. She allowed the facade of happiness to fall away as thoughts of yesterday creeped in. After Derek left the therapy appointment, Alyssa had broken down and shed enough tears to fill a bucket.

Poor Maggie.

She'd acted like she wasn't bothered in the least and talked Alyssa off the ledge. Then, she told her that Derek's abrupt departure was actually a good thing. He was finally feeling. Finally trying to process Katie's death and his own emotional turmoil. She'd advised Alyssa to be patient and was confident he'd come around.

Patience had never been her strong suit.

A knock at the door made her jolt. "I thought I told you to go home, Han. One of us needs to have a social li—Derek!" she said on a gasp as the door swung open revealing the doorway-filling silhouette of her husband.

She shot to her feet on trembling legs. "W-what are you doing here, Derek?"

A large brown paper bag dangled from one hand and a bottle of wine from the other. He looked so unbelievably tempting in dark-wash jeans and a Trident Ink T-shirt stretched across his broad chest. At some point since yesterday, he'd trimmed his beard. It was now cropped close to his jaw, her favorite look on him.

Man, how she wanted to vault over the desk and into his arms, but she wasn't confident enough to do it in that moment. And that was a terrible feeling.

He flashed her a crooked grin. The sexy one. The one that made her knees wobbly, her panties wet, and her lacy bra insufficient at hiding her pebbled nipples. A fact that was not lost on him, if the direction of his gaze was any indication.

He stepped into the room and deposited the items on her desk. With only the desk separating them, he was now close enough to smell. The scent of him was so masculine, so sexy, so familiar.

And so damn arousing.

Instant wet panties.

"Derek? Sorry, gorgeous," he said. "You must have me confused with someone else. The name's Tyler. We met—"

"The other day." Her brows drew down. They were only supposed to do this twice. While the thought of continuing the sexy game had her blood heating, it also meant another encounter where they weren't themselves. Where they were still playing a game instead of being real and dealing with their issues.

For a fraction of a second she considered telling him to drop the act and just be Derek. But he'd been struggling. And he was here, with her. She'd take him however she could get him. Her lips quirked and her sex throbbed. He wanted to play. She could play and save reality for later. "Yes, Tyler, I remember you now. It was the day I had trouble with my hotel room key." They could talk about their issues later. After playtime.

"Really?" he said as he backed up and took the spot on the couch Hannah had vacated. "I suppose it was that day. I like to remember it as the day I ate the sweetest pussy I've ever tasted."

Her knees went from wobbly to complete Jell-O and she gripped the edge of the desk to keep from dropping to the floor. "I remember that too." Her voice was breathy. She needed him so bad.

He quirked a brow and stretched both arms out along the back of the couch. "Seems as though I remember the score being uneven."

Alyssa chuckled. She'd wanted him in her mouth last time, but he hadn't given her the opportunity. This wasn't the time to bring up that the score was uneven because he charged out of the room like his ass was on fire. This was him continuing the game. Showing her he was still in. This was the time to make him as crazy as he'd made her in that hotel room.

"Well," she said, trailing her hand along the top of the desk as she walked around to the front. She perched her bottom on the edge of the desk and crossed her legs at the ankle. "We can't have that, now can we?"

"Get over here," *Tyler* growled.

White-hot desire shot through her. She sauntered forward, swaying her hips until she was about a foot in front of him. "Stand up."

He stared up at her as the seconds ticked by. Ninety percent of the time, Derek was in charge in the bedroom. He liked control, and she liked to give it up to him. But there was no way in hell he was able to hold on to that control while his cock was in her mouth. Alyssa had the power in those moments. And she loved every second of it.

As he rose to his feet, she dropped to her knees between his legs and wasted no time flicking open the button on his jeans and drawing the zipper down. With her eyes locked on his, Alyssa eased the denim down over his hips. Once they cleared his muscular ass, the material pooled on the floor.

The sight of her husband, clad in only a T-shirt and charcoal gray boxer briefs had her closing her eyes and swallowing past a lump in her throat. It had been so long since she had this pleasure.

"Baby," he whispered, his voice rough, needy.

She opened her eyes and smiled up at him. "You are the most amazing man I've ever known," she said.

Something flashed in his eyes. Something that took him out of the intimate moment. Guilt.

Unacceptable.

It wasn't the time for guilt or sorrow. It was time for connection. She drew his boxer briefs down and licked her lips as his long, stiff cock sprang free.

"Jesus, baby," Derek said. "You haven't even touched me and I'm ready to shoot off."

A laugh bubbled up. "Well, think unsexy thoughts or you'll miss the best part."

He grunted. "There isn't a thought in the world unsexy enough to hold me back when you're down on your knees for me."

"Then I guess this is gonna be pretty quick."

He laughed, and her heart surged. Their easy banter and teasing was another of the many things she'd missed. Having it back was a precious gift.

She grasped the back of his calves then slid her hands up slowly, making sure to drag her nails along his skin. He shivered under her touch. When she reached the back of his thighs, she paused and gave her attention to the large tattoo on his right thigh. The day he got it was one she'd never forget.

The ink was a different style than every other piece he wore. Where much of his skin was covered in a mixture of tribal tats, military tats, and colorful ink, this was sketch style. It looked like an artist's rough, somewhat unfinished, pencil sketch. It was a man and a woman locked in a sexual embrace. The man was standing with his hands on the woman's nude ass. Her legs wrapped around his waist, head tilted back in obvious ecstasy. And his face was buried in her breasts. The only way to describe it was erotic.

He'd gotten it the night they got engaged. A tribute to her and their relationship in image form, since he wasn't one for inking names on his skin. The incomplete look of the sketch style represented them as well. Their life together, like the sketch, was unfinished. Never to be completed.

She'd been bowled over when he showed her the design. No one ever saw it but her. Okay, maybe his physician, but it was something special just for them.

That night might as well have been yesterday instead of years ago, the memory was so strong. As she'd watched the tattoo artist ink him, she'd gotten so turned on she almost made herself come just by crossing her legs. Derek had been aware of exactly how affected she'd been by the emerging image. Unfortunately, they couldn't act out the scene with the soreness of fresh ink, but they'd managed to get each other off just the same.

She'd ended up on her knees much as she was now, and he'd come down her throat before lying on his back, dragging her up to his face, and eating her until she'd screamed.

Still one of the best nights of her life.

"That night was hot as fuck," he said as she ran her fingers over the tattoo.

She couldn't speak as the combined barrage of memories and desire brought a surge of emotions to the surface. Tears threatened, but she held them back. Instead, she fisted his cock in her hand and pumped twice before drawing the tip to her mouth. She tongued the slit, then sucked the head into her mouth.

"Fuck," he said on a groan the moment her lips closed around him.

A salty flavor of precum hit her senses, making her moan. She gripped his ass with one hand and cupped his balls with the other as she worked her mouth down his length. It had been a while, but she hadn't forgotten what he liked, so she took him to the back of her throat, hollowed out her cheeks and slid her lips back up to the tip. Then, she repeated the process.

He shoved both hands into her hair, gathering up the strands, and keeping a firm hold on her head. She still set the pace, but he could take over at any time, and the small loss of the upper hand made her pussy clench with need. "Fuck, fuck," he whispered as though talking to himself.

It was hard to keep her lips from curling into a smile, but she managed to keep them locked around his shaft. This time, when he hit the back of her throat, she swallowed.

"Christ, that mouth. You have any idea how beautiful you look right now, baby?"

Pleasure hit her hard. Derek never failed to make her feel like the most gorgeous woman on the planet. She'd been pretty innocent when they'd met, and he'd been on the more experienced end of the spectrum, but from the first time her lips touched him, he'd told her he'd never had better.

That wasn't entirely accurate. He didn't just tell her he'd never had better. He'd made her believe it with every fiber of her being.

And that pretty much made her want him every chance she got.

CHAPTER FIFTEEN

How the hell she did it, Derek would never know. All women had a mouth. All women had tongues. They could all suck, lick, and hum. Yet Alyssa turned a blow job into a fucking art form. It certainly wasn't born of experience, because his had been the one and only cock in her mouth and she had been the best from the first time.

Sure, she got bolder and it got even better with practice, but it had been fucking mind blowing right out of the gate.

And in that moment, with her hot mouth wrapped around his dick, sucking like she wanted to consume him, there was nothing that topped it.

She glided her glistening lips up his length until he nearly popped out of her mouth, then flicked her tongue along the sensitive spot just under the head of his cock at the same time she gave his balls a gentle tug.

Stars shot across his vision, the shock of pleasure so intense it was nearly painful. His hips bucked, and she must have anticipated the reaction because she widened her mouth allowing him to plunge back down her throat.

Tightening his hands in the silky strands of her hair, he held himself deep in her mouth as she swallowed again. Cheeks flushed, eyes glassy, mouth stretched around his girth, she made for one sexy picture.

Sweat popped out across his forehead and his muscles began to twitch. "Shit," he cried out as he yanked himself from her hungry mouth. Another millisecond of that and he'd explode like a rocket launcher. As much as he loved to watch her swallow his cum, tonight nothing would quell the need but her coming on his cock.

"What's wrong?" she asked, chest heaving, and sat back on her heels. "Did I—"

"I need your pussy," he said, yanking her to her feet and spinning her so she faced the desk. "I really need that hot, tight pussy." He gave her upper back a gentle push. "Tits on the desk."

Her breath hitched, and she did as he commanded without a second's hesitation. Fuck, that was a sight. She'd turned her head, so her cheek rested on the desk, palms flat on the surface. The formfitting dress she wore stretched tight across her ass, drawing his attention to one of his favorite parts of her body.

With a heavy touch, he palmed the rounded globes then fisted the clingy material and worked it up over her hips. Two firm, bare ass cheeks separated by a flimsy string of bright red fabric greeted him. "Damn, baby," he said, running his hands over her smooth skin.

He slipped one finger under the fabric of her thong, ran it along the curve of her ass, and gave a tug. She gasped and squirmed as the material pulled taut against her clit.

With a snap of his wrist, he tore the flimsy panties from her and tossed them to the ground. It didn't take but a whisper of a touch to discover his woman was wet. Fucking soaked to be precise.

"Oh my God," she said as he strummed his fingers through her slippery opening.

"You want me," he stated.

"Always," she immediately replied. "All. The. Time."

He closed his eyes and let the words wash over him. "I need you. I'm trying. It's just…this is all I have right now." She deserved more. Deserved him to pour out his soul, but he was still lost in his head.

She turned and met his gaze, her eyes full of the love he'd come to expect from her. He fucking missed that look. "I need you too. I will always need you. This is enough…for now."

That was it. Thankfully she was drenched because foreplay was over. If he wasn't inside her in the next few seconds, he'd start howling at the moon. "Spread," he demanded, impressed there was enough blood going to his brain to make him speak.

Alyssa must have sensed how close to the edge he was riding, because she didn't bother with any teasing or playful quips. All she did was widen her stance and wait, her breath coming in choppy bursts.

"That's good, baby." Her pussy gleamed in the harsh office light. Part of him would love to delve in and lap up all that juice with his tongue, but his cock was in charge and it wouldn't be put off another second.

"Please don't make me wa—" Alyssa screamed as he slammed to the hilt with one powerful thrust. "Yes," she said on a breathy moan. "So perfect."

He couldn't have said it better himself. She was hot, tight, creamy, and soft as silk around his cock. He'd been wrong before. There was one thing better than her mouth, and it was her pussy.

This was exactly where he belonged. It was like coming home. If home was where one went for the hottest, most extreme pleasure imaginable. How had he neglected this part of himself, this part of *them* for so long? He didn't deserve this anymore, but he was just selfish enough to take it.

With each thrust, he increased his speed and force until he was fucking her with a strength that shook the desk. A half-full Styrofoam coffee cup teetered precariously, and papers flew off the desk, littering the floor.

"Oh my God, I love this," Alyssa said between gasps for breath. "Harder, harder."

He gripped her hips with a bruising strength and slammed into her again and again. His balls tightened and felt hot to the point of boiling, but he gritted his teeth and held off the orgasm. No way would he come before feeling her lose control all over his cock.

When he released her hip and fisted her hair, giving a less than gentle tug, Alyssa screamed again. "Derek! Fuck me, Derek!"

Balls-deep inside her, he stilled. She'd screamed his name. His real name. Not some made up name for a game the therapist thought would help them reconnect. His real fucking name. And it was the best goddamned thing he'd ever heard in his entire life.

Two years.

It had been two years since he heard his name shouted in ecstasy. That was wrong on so many levels.

"What happened? Why did you stop?" Her voice was high pitched and breathy, desperate. "Oh shit! I messed it up. I'm sorry." She pushed up on her elbows and tried to look over her shoulder, but he still held her by the hair. "It just felt so good, I didn't think. I should have called you Ty—"

"No!" He used his free hand to slap her ass.

She jumped and let out a half yelp, half moan.

"Never again. I know why we did it, and I know it wasn't real, and I think it even worked, but I never want to hear another man's name when I'm inside you. Ever." He tugged her hair and this time the noise she emitted was all lusty moan. "Got it?"

"Yes," she said, squirming on his dick. The walls of her pussy rubbed all over him and his eyes nearly crossed. "You need to start moving, Derek. I can't take it."

He slapped her ass again and her pussy spasmed around him. Her hips moved like she was trying to fuck herself on his cock, but his pelvis pressed her to the desk limiting her ability to move. "This is my show, baby. Now, say it again."

"Derek," she said.

Slap.

"The whole thing."

"Fuck me, Derek."

Slap.

"Again." He drew his hips back until she whimpered from the loss.

"Fuck me, Derek!" This time she yelled and smacked a palm against the desk.

"Goddamned right I'm gonna fuck you." He rammed back into her and let go of the thin thread of control he'd been clinging to. He fucked her like an animal. Like a wild beast who'd been separated from its mate and had just found her again.

Alyssa gave as good as she got, pushing back into him with every stroke. Cries of pleasure flew from her each time he bottomed out in her pussy.

"I can't hold it back," she said.

Thank God. He was about two seconds from filling her to the brim. "Come, baby. Come now."

He'd barely gotten the words out when her pussy clamped down and she screamed out his name as her body trembled against her desk. The sight of her coming, feel of her squeezing him, and smell of her arousal filling the room overwhelmed him and he finally gave himself over to the monster orgasm. "Fuck, Lyss," he yelled as he spilled deep inside his wife.

Spent, he collapsed on Alyssa's back, dwarfing her with his hulking form. "I'll let you breathe in a second, baby. Your pussy sucked out all my energy."

Beneath him, she chuckled. "I like the feel of you on me."

With a grunt, he forced himself to rise and pressed kisses along her spine. "Maybe when we're in a bed, but it can't feel good to have two hundred twenty-five pounds of man squashing you against the wood."

He helped her up and spun her, drawing her into his arms for a deep kiss.

Minutes later, when they came up for air, she said, "Hi, Derek." Love shone from her eyes clear as day. There wasn't a hint of anger over the way he left the therapist's office. Too bad what he had to say would probably extinguish that light. Guilt hit him square in the gut.

"Hey, Lyss. Have I told you how much I like your desk?"

"Ha, once or twice, big guy."

He snorted. "Yeah, guess it's not the first time we made use of it, huh?"

She slipped her hands under the shirt he still wore and coasted them up and down the ridges of his abs. "Not sure there's a piece of furniture we own between our house, the shop, and my office that we haven't broken in. What's in the bag?"

"Chinese."

"Oh man, you must have read my mind. I'm starved." She scraped a manicured nail over his nipple and he groaned.

It should have been impossible with the way he just came, but her small hands roaming all over his skin had his cock twitching against her stomach. If she kept at it much longer, she'd find herself right back over the desk.

If he knew his wife, she wouldn't utter a word of complaint. In fact, he probably wouldn't get the chance to bend her over again. She was likely to shove him down on the couch, climb on, and ride him to exhaustion.

Sounded damned good to him.

As much as he wanted that exact scenario to play out in more than just his head, he'd been selfish enough for one night.

They had too much to talk about. And when it was over, she just might slap him across his face and let him know what he already knew.

A knife pierced his heart. Christ, if his actions caused him this pain, he could only imagine what he was doing to her.

He was a bastard.

So, instead of letting the fantasy unwind, he gently removed her hands from his abdomen. "Why don't you go get cleaned up while I unpack it. We can eat on the couch."

She beamed at him then headed for the private bathroom attached to her office. With her dress bunched around her waist and her panties a shredded mess on the floor, he was treated to a view of her twitching ass as she walked away from him.

Damn, his wife was one blessed lady. He wolf-whistled at her and she turned and winked before disappearing into the bathroom.

When the door clicked shut, he set about unpacking the cartons of food and pouring two glasses of Alyssa's favorite Chardonnay.

Now that his temptation of a wife was out of view, guilt hit him hard. Fucking her over the desk hadn't been part of his plan for the evening. He'd just come to talk. But once he'd seen her in that boner-inducing dress that hugged every curve and teased with just a hint of cleavage, he'd been helpless to do anything else.

There was so much they had to work out. So many words of apology that he owed her. Especially after the way he acted the last two times they were together. He'd meant to say all those words before touching her.

But then he'd seen her and all his good intentions were shot to hell. Damn it, he just craved his wife. Plain and simple.

Simple.

Fuck. Nothing about their marriage was simple at the moment.

CHAPTER SIXTEEN

Alyssa smoothed her hands over the wild strands of her hair then glared at her image in the mirror. They'd done it again. Sex without a condom. For the past few days, she'd been forcing herself to think of anything but the possibility of pregnancy, not that it worked. The worry was on her mind constantly. Until Derek walked in and got her all hot and bothered. Then it was easy. Then all rational thought fell straight out of her brain.

Damn it.

She rolled her eyes toward the ceiling. Maybe there'd be some divine inspiration up there.

Nope.

She had to keep it light in her head, the thoughts of being pregnant. Because if she allowed it to truly seep in, she'd go into full panic mode at the thought of bringing another child into the world. Another child that she'd love with every fiber of her being. Another child that could get hurt or sick and be lost to her yet again.

A low moan filled the bathroom as the pain of Katie's passing washed over her.

She had to tell Derek. It wasn't fair of her to keep it from him.

Instead of stalling any longer, she gave her reflection a harsh stare and tossed her long hair into a messy bun on top of her head. The style made her look young, which in fact, she still was. Lately, she'd been feeling aged beyond her years.

Tragedy did that to a person.

She shook off the maudlin thoughts, straightened her dress, and flicked off the light while reaching for the door. Derek sat on the couch, jeans back in place, staring into a Chinese takeout carton. Kung Pao Chicken was her guess. And for her, he'd have gotten—

"Oh hey." He glanced up and blinked. "Didn't even hear the door open. Must be losing my edge. Here, I got you shrimp lo mein."

Her favorite.

"Thanks." She accepted the carton and disposable chopsticks as she sank onto the leather couch. Without panties, she felt a little drafty and curled her legs underneath her bottom. Facing Derek, her knees rested against his thigh.

How many nights over the years had they sat this very same way? First on the sofa at either his or her apartment. Then in the apartment they shared together. And finally, in the home they'd purchased shortly after getting married. Nights like this were her absolute favorite.

They'd eat, chat about their day, touch, kiss. Eventually the caresses would turn heated and they'd abandon the food in favor of tasting each other. Sometimes it was sweet, loving, slow. Others it was a mad frenzy of desire and need. But always, it ended in an explosion of pleasure for both of them—usually more than once for her.

She was pretty certain Katie was conceived on one of those perfect nights.

She had to say something. But the words just wouldn't come.

It was ridiculous, really. She didn't have a clue, not a symptom, or a sign, or a feeling that she was pregnant. It was way, way too early. But she was freaking out nonetheless. Confessing the possibility of pregnancy to her unflappable man would help. He'd stay rational, calm, and talk her off the ledge like he was so adept at doing.

"Mmm, this hit the spot," she said as the salty flavor of the noodles flooded her senses. "I feel like I could inhale this whole thing in under three minutes. Care to challenge me?"

Narrowed eyes met her gaze. "What's with the voice?"

"Huh," she asked.

"You sound weird. Like falsely cheerful."

With a sigh she could almost feel weighing her down, she stuck the chopsticks in the carton and gave Derek her full attention. "I cut my foot a few weeks ago."

His focus shifted to her foot. "Shit. You okay? Should you be walking on it?"

"Oh, no it's fine." She waved away his concern. "It was a tiny scratch. I was wearing socks in the garage and stepped on a nail. Yes, I know it was stupid to be barefoot in there, but I was in a rush. And it was supposed to be a quick run in and run out. But then I couldn't find what I was looking for, so I was rummaging around."

Great, now she was babbling about her shoes.

"Uh, anyway, the nail was filthy, so a doctor gave me an antibiotic just to make sure it didn't get infected."

Concern marred his face and he'd stopped eating as well. "But it's okay now, right?"

"Yes, totally fine. Barely even bothered me." Her voice wavered, and she almost lost her nerve. The door to her office beckoned. She could run before the words were said.

Not that she ever would.

"Sooo…" Derek prompted.

"So antibiotics can weaken birth control pills and make them ineffective." It came out as a whisper.

Derek's eyes widened, and his mouth opened and closed no less than four times. "Holy…uh…fuck. Are you…"

She shook her head so hard the room wobbled. "Way too early to tell."

"Jesus, I'm not ready for that. I can't even process it." He scrubbed a hand over his bearded face. "This can't be happening, Lyss. Not now. Not after all we've been through. What if…" He shook his head.

Well, crap. Now her mind was spiraling out of control with a million unwelcome thoughts and worries. Derek was supposed to remain calm. He was supposed to hold her and tell her not to worry, that they'd get through it. They couldn't both panic. He had to be calm, rational, steady. It was how they worked as a couple.

She reached for his hand, but he pulled away, stood, and paced the floor of her office.

Her rejected heart sank, but she didn't say anything. She'd had a few days to obsess about this and wasn't handling the idea of it well herself. It wasn't fair to expect him to react any better.

While she waited for him to right his mind, she picked up her food and shoveled a few bites into her mouth. Anything to pass the time.

After about five solid minutes of watching him attempt to wear a hole through her office carpet, she couldn't stand another second of the thick quiet. "Der? Hey, Derek? Can we talk about this?"

The eyes that met hers were not the eyes of a satisfied husband who just had desk-rattling sex. They were the eyes of a tortured man fighting an enemy. The invisible kind. The kind that brewed in one's own mind. The absolute worst kind of foe. She'd seen those eyes before. Years ago, when they'd first met, and Derek had struggled with PTSD. If only she could utilize some of the tools that helped him back then.

The food in her mouth suddenly felt like paste and she swallowed the unappetizing lump. It might as well have been a jagged rock, the way it seemed to tear her insides as it traveled to her stomach. A stomach that threatened to reject everything she'd just consumed. Whatever he was about to say wasn't going to be good. She could feel it in her bones.

"Sometimes I wish you'd known me back when I was a SEAL," he said.

Her eyebrows drew down and she stuck the chopsticks in the carton before placing it on the desk. They never talked about his SEAL days. Not anymore. Where was he going with this? What was eating at him so bad that he'd revisit dark days? "I would have liked to have known you then." She tilted her head. "Maybe I could have helped spare you some of the pain you went through."

It was something she'd thought about a lot when they first got together. Had they been introduced three, even two years prior, would she have been able to spare him some of the anguish and suffering he'd endured?

He grunted. "No, you didn't know me back then, but you sure got stuck cleaning up the mess, didn't you?"

"Baby," she said, snagging his hand and pulling him back down to the couch. Then she threw her leg over his and settled on his lap, straddling him. Her hands framed his face and she tilted his head up to meet her gaze. "I never, not once, thought of it that way. Everyone has issues, and I never resented helping you through yours. I was honored to have the job."

His strong hands settled on her waist as a sad smile crossed his face. They felt good there. As though it hadn't been so long since he held her like this. Since they had the simple intimacy of talking without any thought for personal space. "I know, baby. And that's not even where I'm going with this."

"Okay, so why don't you tell me why you brought it up?"

He nodded. "As a SEAL, we worked in teams. And we trained…a lot. We were forever training. No matter how good we got, how strong we were, how fast. We could always be better, stronger, faster. So we trained. And we trained. And we trained. Every damn day."

She nodded and moved her hands to his chest. This was nothing new. He'd told her about his training. And she'd done her own research. Even watched a multi-episode documentary on BUDs training back when they first met, and she was eager to soak up any information she could have in her quest to understand him.

"When it came time for a mission, we planned down to the very last detail. Then made backup plans. And contingencies for our back up plans. There was no problem too big. No obstacle we weren't willing or able to tackle. But we always did it the smart way. With knowledge, skill, and planning."

He tightened his fingers on her waist and she remained silent. Whatever this was, he needed to get it out.

"When we were certain we had every viable possibility accounted for, we went in as a team. And we were successful. Almost every time. Because we had to be. There were only two options. Success or failure. And failure meant death. Failure meant someone's family didn't get to see them again. Failure meant pain and loss. Failure was final. There were no do overs. I was in charge of my team. I was in charge of their success and protection. You know how seriously I took that and how fucked up I was over the few times we didn't succeed."

With each sentence, his tone grew darker and his eyes flatter. Alyssa's stomach began to hurt. Her husband was in pain. Serious, soul-crushing pain.

"You are my team now. It's my responsibility to protect you. To make you happy. And it was my responsibility to do the same for our daughter. So when Katie was diagnosed, we planned. And we attacked. Hard." His voice cracked. "But it failed. And she died."

Tears flooded Alyssa's eyes, but she didn't bother to stem them. This needed to happen. Actually, this needed to happen a year ago, but she would take it now.

"And then I just kept on failing."

Huh? Alyssa frowned.

"I abandoned the rest of my team. I let you down. I let you suffer because I couldn't handle what happened to our little girl. I left you behind."

"Derek—"

He shook his head. "Just let me say it all. Please."

"Okay," she whispered. A feeling of dread overtook her. This wasn't going to end well. She could feel it deep in her gut.

He hung his head and stared at his lap. "You deserve a man, a husband, who won't check out when things get hard. I wasn't that man. And now, with the chance that you might be pregnant, what was my first thought again? To flee. To let you down all over again."

That was enough. Time to take control of this conversation before it went off the rails. "Derek," she said. "Derek, look at me, please."

He lifted his gaze. "Have you noticed how many people have quoted the divorce rate for couples after the loss of a child?" When he didn't reply, she forged on. "A lot of people. And you want to know why? It's because what happened to us is horrible. Beyond horrible. It's unnatural. Parents shouldn't have to b-bury their children." A sob stuck in her throat, but she forced it down. Later she could cry her eyes out. For once, her husband needed her to be the strong one, so that's what she'd do.

She ran her hand over his soft beard and said in a whisper, "It's the worst thing a couple can go through. And it tears them apart. Now, I love you, and I think you are the most amazing man in the world. But I do not think you are super human. I do not think you are the one man on earth who can experience what we did and remain unaffected and, well, un-fucked up.

"I think the only thing that either of us has done wrong over the past year is to think that our relationship was above breaking. We're human, just like every other couple. Maybe if we hadn't been so cocky, we'd have gotten help sooner and wouldn't have wasted so much time apart from each other. Maggie told me yesterday that now all we're doing is throwing away more time on misguided guilt.

"And don't you think my first thought was to run away as well? Pretty natural when facing something as scary as a pregnancy. But we didn't run. We're here, talking."

"I can't, Lyss. I'm too eaten up with it. The guilt. You need someone who isn't going to let you down. Someone who is strong enough to handle your fears and worries as well as his own. I don't know if that is me anymore." Gently, he scooped her off his lap and deposited her on the couch next to him.

Before she had the chance to react, he'd stood and moved toward the door. There was a heaviness in his step. Alyssa had seen him down and out before. Not often, but he'd suffered some issues with PTSD when they first met. This was different though. This was the walk of a terrified man, and for the first time, real fear chilled her blood.

Nothing she said got through to him. And now he was leaving.

"I need some time," he said when he reached the door.

"Time for what?" Despite how she tried to be strong, her voice wavered.

"Time to sort out my head. It's hard enough trying to find a way to forgive myself for being unable to save Katie. Now I have to add the possibility of another child to my list of worries. I'm not sure I can give you what you need anymore."

She stood as well. "Don't you think I get to make that decision? About what I need?"

"I love you, Lyss."

"I know." And she did. That wasn't the issue here. The issue was whether or not he could deal with his grief. Because it had turned into guilt, and if he couldn't deal with it, their marriage might be over. "I love you too, Derek. And I need you. Just you."

"We'll see," he said as he walked out the door.

It was as though he took all the air in the room with him when he left. The air and her strength. Her knees buckled, and she collapsed to the couch, a pain in her chest she'd only felt one other time. The moment she realized her little girl wouldn't be waking up. Now she might be facing her second horrifying loss.

She'd been filled with such a strong sense of hope when he'd had waltzed into her office earlier. Finally, they were going to connect as Derek and Alyssa and begin the process of moving past their pain, past their grief and guilt, past their loss.

Watching him turn his back and walk away was so much harder this time around. Now she knew what was going on in his head. Knew the demons he was battling were great. But she would help him with those demons. She'd done it before. They'd done it before. Together as a couple.

The taste of him still lingered on her tongue and she licked her bottom lip as though trying to catch any stray molecule of his essence.

And then the anger came. Not for what had happened in the time since Katie passed. But for what happened tonight. For what happened the last time they were together. She'd made it clear that she wanted to fight for their relationship and was willing to get just about any kind of help she could.

But Derek just kept walking out. The Derek she knew and loved wasn't a quitter. He was a gutter fighter when there was something he felt passionately about.

Maybe that was just it. Maybe all of this, the pain, guilt, fear, and now potential to experience it all over again with a new life, maybe it had snuffed out his desire to fight for them.

Oh, God.

Her stomach pitched, and she dashed back into the bathroom, falling to her knees just in time to lose everything she'd eaten.

With a trembling hand, she wiped her mouth and pressed her fingers to her lips.

He'd come back to her. They'd vowed to remain together.

Through good times and bad.

Sickness and health.

Until death parted them.

But it was supposed to be their own death, not something even worse. Not the death of their child.

With her tattered heart aching, Alyssa slumped against the wall of the bathroom and sobbed for all she'd lost and all she still might lose.

CHAPTER SEVENTEEN

"You gonna offer Thea the job?" Derek finished wiping down his station as he called across the shop to Brett. He'd just finished working on Hunter's piece and needed one more session to get it all wrapped up. He'd thrown himself into work the past few days. It was self-preservation, the only time he got some kind of break from torturing himself. If he wasn't working, he was obsessing.

Obsessing over his relationship with Alyssa. Obsessing over the possibility of having another child. Obsessing over his own guilt.

With a grunt, Brett fished around in the refrigerator. "The ink on her certificate is barely dry," he said into the fridge. "You want a beer?"

Derek moved to the sink and filled his hands with soap. He'd popped in for about a third of Thea's interview and was impressed with what he knew of her so far. She may not have been piercing long but she had drive and personality. Two major checks in the plus column.

"Thanks. Grab some juice for Hunter, too. He's waiting for us in the breakroom. And I know she's brand new, but she seems like she'd fit in well. And she's eager to prove herself. That's always a bonus. You could start her with easy clients and train her for a bit on the more difficult piercings."

Brett snickered. "I could train her on a few things all right," he called over his shoulder as he walked into the breakroom.

"Stop right there!" Derek jogged after him and joined Brett and Hunter at the round table staff ate at daily. He grabbed one of the beers and a bottle opener. "You will not touch her, flirt with her, tease her, or propose to her. Hell, I don't really even want you to look at her. She'll be your employee and nothing more. You get me?"

"Thanks for the lecture, but I'm pretty sure I can control myself. Let's talk about you instead. You done being a complete and total asshole yet?" Brett leaned back in his chair and fixed Derek with his meanest scowl.

Hunter just took in the show without a word, one brow arched well into his forehead. Being a customer and all, he didn't typically hang out with them, but tonight Derek had worked on his ink long after the shop closed. Brett's workday had ended hours ago, but he'd hung around, having a rare dateless night, shooting the shit as Derek worked and Hunter zoned out.

It was nearing midnight and Derek wasn't looking forward to returning to an impersonal hotel room. Killing some more time with his buddies was no hardship. Unless Brett planned on heckling him some more about the way he was screwing up his marriage.

"Can we not do this now?" he asked, returning Brett's scowl and upping him one ounce of pissed off. It had been two days since the debacle in Alyssa's office and Brett hadn't missed an opportunity to cram his opinion down Derek's throat.

"Sorry, bro. Act like an asshole and you'll be treated as such." He drained his beer and turned his attention to Hunter. "You see, Derek here has one of the most amazing women in the world as his wife. She's not only hot as fuck—" Derek growled, and Brett shot him a wide toothy grin. "—she's sweet as pie, smart as a whip, and she'd lay down her life for this POS," he said jerking a thumb in Derek's direction.

"If that's not bad enough, they fuck like freakin' bunnies even after being married for so long. Never made any kinda sense. You mention the word sex in front of Lyss and she blushes like you caught her nekkid." He shook his head. "Yet I happen to know for a fact that that woman—"

"Okay, I think he gets it, Brett."

Brett had been half in love with Alyssa from the moment he met her. Mostly it was a familial kind of love, but there were a few times in the beginning where Derek was convinced Brett would scoop her up for himself if he fucked it up. While Brett acted like being in a monogamous relationship was akin to catching the plague, he never failed to let Derek now just how lucky a bastard he was.

Growing up, Brett had the shittiest examples of relationships. Made sense he'd be fascinated by a strong one. Or what used to be a strong one.

"I've met her," Hunter said with a nod. "Seems like a keeper." Hunter wasn't one to pry or offer unsolicited advice and Derek appreciated it. The man knew pain. Knew suffering. He fought the good fight everyday just to keep moving forward.

"She is. Wouldn't know it by the way D's been treating her," Brett said, causing Derek's blood to heat. He'd had about enough of his friend's two cents. What the fuck did Brett know about making it last with someone for more than a week or two?

Not a goddamned thing.

He opened his mouth, prepared to blast Brett for running his trap about something he knew shit about.

"Was married once," Hunter said.

Both he and Brett stopped shooting eye-lasers at each other and listened. Since Hunter wasn't one to wax poetic, whenever he spoke, it was usually something important.

"You're pretty young for a married once situation," Brett said.

Hunter snorted. "Was even younger when I got hitched. Twenty." He shook his head as shadows flashed in his eyes. "Seems like another lifetime now. She was a keeper too.

Beautiful girl. Loved life. Loved me. And fuck, did I love her. So many guys in the teams, their wives cheated, couldn't handle the pressure, fucked up the finances while they were overseas. You guys heard all the stories. Not Beth. First time I was injured— shot in three places—she gave me exactly what I needed. Softness when it was called for, a good swift kick in the ass at times too. But always love."

He fell silent. There was a point to this story, a point Derek both wanted and dreaded hearing. Because it wasn't going to have a happy ending and it was for his benefit. "What happened?" he forced himself to ask.

Hunter sighed and scratched his chin. "Well, I on the other hand thought I wasn't what she needed. I thought she could find better. A man who wasn't in danger all the time. Who didn't leave at the drop of a hat for who the hell knew how long. One who wouldn't come home all shot up. Who didn't get a little more fucked in the head with each mission."

He finished his juice then set up a shot and fired the cup across the breakroom into the trash can.

"Nice shot," Brett said. "So, I'm guessing you left your girl."

"Sure did." Hunter shook his head. "Biggest fucking mistake of my life. Knew it the second the words came out of my mouth, but I was too fucked up to make it right. Not sure whose heart I crushed more, hers or my own." He sighed, a deep remorseful sound. "Found out about year and a half later she was engaged again. Guy turned out to be a real fuckwad. Tell you what, if I had it to do over again, I would have held on to her real tight."

He rose and extended a hand to Derek. "Thanks for staying late, man. Appreciate you accommodating me."

"Happy to do it," Derek said as he shook Hunter's hand. "See you in two weeks. Should be the last session."

Hunter nodded and walked toward the door. His gait was so smooth, if Derek didn't know it, he'd never guess the guy had a prosthetic limb.

Derek and Brett exchanged a look. Was that it? His girl married a fuckwad? There had to be more to the story.

When Hunter reached the glass door, he turned around and pierced Derek with a cold, hard stare. "He beat her," he said. "Never knew or I'd have ripped his nuts out through his throat. Pushed her down the stairs. Broken neck, head injury. She survived three days in a coma before she died. We're all fucked in our own way, Derek. Don't know what's in your head, but I figure you're here now instead of home with your woman so it can't be good. Hope you ain't thinking of bailing, man. You think maybe she needs something you can't give her? Trust me, she don't. Shit's gonna happen that you can't control or stop. And it's gonna feel like it's tearing you apart. But believe me, getting the chance to try to control shit, even if it fails, it beats sitting on the sideline any day."

With that, Hunter stepped out into the night leaving Derek feeling like he'd just been kicked in the stomach.

"Shit," Brett said running a hand down his face, his usual smirk nowhere to be found. "It's a fucking miracle that guy's not rocking back and forth in the corner."

"Yeah." Hunter's words hit him hard. The man was right. Shit was going to happen. As SEALS, they knew it better than most. How many innocent lives had he witnessed destroyed by war and evil?

Too many to count.

Even here, in the land of the free, horrific things happened on a daily basis. Out of his control. Incurable disease, mass shootings, car accidents. This list went on. He could toss away his life with Alyssa on the paranoid notion that something might happen. Or he could man the fuck up, protect her from what he did have control over, and enjoy the rest of his days with her.

Seemed so easy when he broke it down like that. Easy to say, harder to live when there was a voice in his head telling him he should have protected his family better. Should have fought harder, should have found a way to make Katie better.

"There's a chance Lyss is pregnant," he blurted before he thought the better of it. Brett would keep his confidence, if she was in fact pregnant.

Brett didn't even try to hide his surprise. His eyes bugged, and his mouth flapped like his jaw came unhinged "Whoa, I had no idea you were ready for that. I didn't even realize you guys were talking much, let alone fucking."

Derek shot his friend a death glare. "We're working on our shit, but there's no way we're ready to even consider having another kid. Way too much baggage to sort through."

"Well you better get ready." Brett grabbed the empty beer bottles and walked them to the recycling can.

Get ready? Really? That was his best friend's advice? "Thanks, B, super helpful."

"Look," Brett said as he planted his palms on the table opposite Derek and leaned forward. "Not saying it's easy, but if she is pregnant, then you have no choice but to find a way to deal with it because it will be your new reality. Think of it like a mission. Unexpected shit happens all the time. Adjust and adapt." He shrugged. "You'll figure it out. Let's go."

He started for the door.

"Where we going?"

"You're going home. I'm going to Jessica's."

"Home? I'm not sure—"

"Okay, D, I'm gonna give it to you straight, okay?" Brett turned and was sporting a seriously pissed off expression. "I can't imagine what it was like for you to lose your baby girl like you did. Fuck, it damn near wrecked me, and I'm just the favorite uncle. So maybe I have no right to give advice, but I love you and I love Lyss, so I'm gonna.

"That woman loves you and would do damn near anything to fix what's broken between you. Including spilling her guts about your sex life to a stranger when she can barely say the word sex in mixed company. You need time to think, process, get your head on straight? Fine. Take that time. But take it at home, with your wife and keep her in the loop every step of the way. Because if you lose her, I'll kick your ass until there's nothing left of you. Get me?"

His buddy's words, combined with Hunter's story, hit him deep. Brett was right. Bottom line was he loved his wife. Despite feeling like he failed her, he wasn't going to leave her. He pretty much couldn't leave her, not if he wanted to survive. That's how much he needed her.

So he'd take Brett's advice and go home to the place where the person who was most vital to him was waiting for him to get his shit together. Not that he was close to that point, but he was working on it. And he'd work harder. And he'd involve Lyss in his healing process.

Jesus, he'd been a fool. Home was where he should have been all along. "Okay. Let's go."

With a snort, Brett slow-clapped. "'Bout fucking time, bro. You better stop for some flowers if you want her to open the door. Maybe a chocolate bar the size of your head."

Shit. He was probably right. Lyss was bound to be pretty pissed at him. "Think I'll get one the size of my dick instead. It'll be bigger."

Brett barked out a laugh. "Good to hear you joking again, man. Welcome back to the land of the living."

She'd let him back; that wasn't a concern. She'd made it clear she wanted to put a tourniquet on their bleeding relationship. Most likely she'd make him grovel a bit, but groveling was easy. He could swallow his pride and grovel like a fucking Olympic champ. Especially if it ended with him and Lyss back in their bed, together, writhing and sweaty.

But Brett was right. He should at least grab some flowers. Groveling combined with a little romance was sure to do the trick. Lyss loved the fuck out of daisies.

He snagged his leather jacket from a hook on the wall and made it halfway to the exit before calling out, "Wait, Jesus. Where am I gonna get flowers at midnight?"

With a laugh, Brett grabbed his own jacket and clapped Derek on the back. "Clearly you don't piss your wife off enough. If you did, you'd know that Farhad actually carries some decent flowers. I'll come with. Could use some mocha goodness before I head to Jessica's."

"Jessica? Who the hell is Jessica?" Derek asked as he followed Brett out of the building.

"Some co-ed at Georgetown. She just texted. Popped her ink cherry last week. Butterfly tramp stamp. Girl's got tits for days." He held his hands out in front of his chest and waggled his eyebrows.

"Christ, B, you seriously banging a college girl with a butterfly tat? Aren't you getting tired of that shit? Another year and you'll officially be a lech." As they walked, he shrugged into his jacket and zipped it against the cold. DC didn't get much snow, but it still got plenty chilly in the winter. "And what the hell do you know about buying flowers for a woman? You don't keep 'em long enough to buy 'em dinner, let alone flowers."

"Pfft. First off, yes, I'm fucking her. No, I'm not tired of it. I'm at least three to five years from becoming a lech, and just because I'm not serious about them doesn't mean I don't treat them right." He pulled open the convenience store door and waved at the older man who looked their way when the door jingled. "I'll have you know I've purchased many a flower. Fuck you very much."

Derek wasn't convinced. Brett put on a good show, but come on. They were in their upper thirties. Who still liked bed hopping at that age?

Just as they stepped into the warm store, LL Cool Jay's *Doin' It* blared from Brett's phone. It was his signature ringtone for all his ladies. He shot Derek a Cheshire grin and pushed the door open again. "Be right back, bro. Looks like the lovely Jessica is getting antsy. Who can blame her when she's waiting on all this?" He winked and slipped back outside with a, "Hey, sugar," for his phone.

Derek rolled his eyes and waved at Farhad who was on his cell behind the counter before strolling to a refrigerated case at the back of the store. With the number of times he visited the store each week, it was hard to believe he'd forgotten the case of colorful flowers in the back.

A surprisingly full and artfully arranged bouquet of pink, yellow, and orange gerbera daisies rested front and center in the case. Perfect. Lyss would love them. She always got the same smile when he bought her flowers or surprised her in any way, really. It was almost sheepish, like she didn't think she deserved the small gift. Made him love buying presents for her.

The moment his fist closed around the metal door handle, the hairs on the back of his neck surged to full attention. Years of SEAL training and countless missions had honed his instincts and taught him to trust his gut.

Every time.

Something was off, and his body knew it.

Holding as still as possible, he shifted his focus from the flowers to the store's reflection in the glass case. His eyes widened and without a thought, training kicked in, and he dropped silent to the floor.

Just thirty feet away, a terrified Farhad stared down the barrel of a rifle held by a masked gunman.

CHAPTER EIGHTEEN

Well, fuck. Looked like he wasn't getting home to Alyssa anytime soon. While the idea of ducking behind some shelves and waiting until Farhad handed over whatever the gunman requested was probably the smartest and safest thing to do, there was no way in hell Derek could live with himself if he cowered like a pussy.

First off, Farhad didn't deserve to be robbed, threatened, or even scared for one millisecond. Poor guy had been through enough with his wife sick at home. Every penny he made went toward her treatment and Derek would be damned if he let some punk asshole run off with even one of those pennies.

Then there was the fact that he was perfectly capable of taking out this larcenous bastard. After many years of planning and executing covert missions, Derek had developed the ability to size up his enemy in an instant. About five-foot-ten and on the scrawny side, the gunman shouldn't pose any kind of serious physical threat. Sure, size wasn't everything, especially when it came to someone with hand-to-hand combat skill, but Derek had both size and training, so he wasn't worried.

What was worrisome was the hunting rifle aimed at a trembling Farhad. A Ruger bolt-action if he wasn't mistaken. Not knowing the masked gunman's abilities with the weapon or how twitchy his trigger finger was made charging him a stupid idea. At least not until he pointed that weapon somewhere else.

"Hands where I can see 'em, old man. Now! Can't have you setting off any silent alarms." His voice held just a hint of a tremor, like he wasn't quite confident. That could be both good and deadly.

Crouched as much as his oversized body would allow, Derek duck-walked along the back edge of the store until he was at the end of the aisle farthest from the assailant. With a stealth born of countless hours of grueling drills, he worked his way to the front of the lane. When he peeked around the shelves, he had an unobstructed view of the gunman and terrified store owner. The attacker's attention was fully rooted on Farhad, so he was completely unaware of Derek's presence.

"Empty the register," the thief commanded, motioning to the register with the gun. "Safe too. I know there's one under the counter." He tossed a tan sack on the checkout counter.

"I-I don't k-know the com-combination." Eyes wide and glassy, Farhad's outstretched arms were visibly shaking.

Jesus. Why the hell did unqualified people try to play hero? The old guy was going to get himself killed trying to save whatever cash was in the safe. Anger heated Derek's veins. That money was so important to Farhad and his family, he was willing to lie to the gunman to protect it.

Derek felt for the man, he really did, but it still wasn't the smart move. Give the fucking thief what he wanted. What was a few thousand dollars compared to Farhad's life? Who would take care of his wife if he was killed in a store robbery gone bad?

"Don't bullshit me, Grandpa. This ain't my first rodeo. Gun's loaded and I have no problem using it." The gun was tucked neatly into his shoulder, one hand on the barrel and one on the trigger. Those arms showed no signs of tiring. The man knew his way around a firearm. "Open the fucking safe. Fill the bag."

Do it! Derek tried to send a mental message to Farhad.

"O-okay," Farhad said. Sweat dotted his brow and trickled down his round face, which turned an unhealthy shade of red. All Derek needed was for him to keel over from a heart attack.

Escapades

Farhad got to work emptying the cash register into the bag. With the way people preferred plastic to paper these days, there couldn't be much more than a few hundred bucks in the register. Hardly seemed worth the risk of a prison stent. Now the safe, that would be a different story. Depending on how diligent Farhad was about making deposits, there could be a few thousand in there.

The street was clearly visible through the windowed front of the shop, but being midnight on a Wednesday, the area was vacant.

Across the street, Brett yammered away into his phone, his back to the convenience store. Derek whipped out his own phone and fired a *call nine-one-one and don't text back* text to Brett. If the gunman heard the vibration, Derek would forfeit the element of surprise and possibly even his life.

Unfortunately, Brett was so involved in his phone call with Jessica of the butterfly tattoo, he completely ignored the incoming text alert. Motherfucker. Derek would be sure to kick his buddy's ass for that later.

That was if he got out of this alive and in one piece.

Alyssa was home, possibly pregnant, and unaware of the danger to him. No way in hell could he go out like this, with his marriage a mess. Nor could he live with himself if he let this asshole walk away with money Farhad had worked his ass off for. Money he'd earned by spending time away from his sick wife.

Shit.

What a clusterfuck.

While Derek was pretty certain he could take out the gunman if he'd just shift his focus from the register for a second, there was a small chance shit would hit the fan and he'd be injured, or worse, killed. What he needed was a good distraction.

But, Christ, if things went belly up, he'd be leaving in a body bag, having never fixed his relationship with Alysa. That thought had his gut churning with regret. If he got out of this alive, not a day would go by where Lyss didn't know she was the most important piece of his world. A minute wouldn't pass where she didn't feel cherished, loved, and pleasured. Definitely pleasured. Because let's face it, he was gonna need a good, hard fuck to work the adrenaline out of his system after this.

After what seemed like hours, but was probably no longer than sixty seconds, Farhad had the register emptied. He raised his hands to head-level once again and cleared his throat. "I n-need to b-bend d-down for the s-s-safe."

"Do it," the assailant said. "And hurry the fuck up." His right leg bounced like there was a spring in his shoe.

Nervous.

That could be deadly depending on how likely he was to clench his hand and fire at Farhad.

Farhad disappeared behind the counter and Derek tensed. This was his chance. All he needed was Farhad to remain hidden below the counter for thirty seconds and he'd have the gunman neutralized.

With a deep breath, Derek grabbed two cans off the closest shelf. Silent as a whisper, he made his way toward the gunman, still in a crouch.

Halfway to the gunman, out in the open, and just about to lob the cans toward the back of the store, a whimper caught both his and the masked man's attention. Huddled behind a Trojan condom display opposite Derek's position, two teenage girls huddled, crying. Fucking shitty parents letting their kids roam the streets of DC in the middle of a school night.

Jesus, he sounded like an old man.

Derek froze as the assailant swiveled toward the girls.

A redhead with long braids sobbed and held her friend. "P-please," she said in a stuttered cry. "Please don't hurt us." Black mascara ran down her pale face much in the same way snot was running from her nose. "Please l-let us go!" She wailed so loud it was difficult to think.

"Shut up!" the gunman screamed. "Just shut the fuck up or I'll shut you up."

The volume of her panic lessened, but she still cried like her tears would somehow save her.

Next to the hysterical teen, her pixie-haired brunette friend stared straight at Derek. Her dark eyes were bug-wide and giant tears streamed silently down her face. Derek shook his head once and pointed to the gunman.

Somehow the girl knew what he was trying to convey, and she shifted her attention to the masked man.

"Get the fuck down. Flat on the ground!"

The silent one obeyed immediately, but the other was so hysterical, she seemed to miss what he'd ordered. "I said get the fuck down."

As the attacker screamed at the girls, Farhad straightened. The gun swung in a wide arc, back and forth between the counter and the girls. With the criminal's attention divided, and him seeming near panic, Derek had to act. He crept closer and just as he was about to lunge for the assailant, the hysterical teen's eyes shifted to him.

And the robber noticed.

"The fuck you lookin' at?" he screamed as he did an about face. There wasn't any time. Not even a fraction of a second for Derek to react. Because if there had been, he would have charged. But the gunman fired off a round the very instant he turned.

Derek was so close to him, the impact of the bullet sent him flying backward. A fiery lance of pain seared the upper left side of his body, stealing his breath and clouding his vision. He crashed into a stacked soup display, smacking the back of his head on God knew what. Stars circled his vision while the girls' screams mixed with the clunking of metal cans as they rained all around, and on him.

"Oh shit, oh fuck!" The gunman's shrill screeches sounded, and all hell broke loose.

Derek's head throbbed in time with his left shoulder. The room swam as his vision tunneled. He fought to remain conscious in the chaos that erupted. Noise came from every direction, cops screaming at the gunman to lower his weapon, crying from teenagers, and shouts about the man that had been shot. That had to be him.

Then, suddenly, the racket faded into the background and the pain receded, replaced by a comforting warmth in his chest.

Alyssa. She was there.

A beautiful cheerful smile on her face, she reached for him. He hadn't seen that look of unguarded joy on her face in two years. Not since the day Katie was diagnosed. He'd kill to put that expression of happiness back on her face. And now he'd never get the chance to see it in person.

"Derek? Fuck. Stay with me, Der. Keep your eyes open. You gotta stay awake so you can kiss that pretty wife of yours. I'll call her. She'll meet us at the hospital. All you gotta do is stay the fuck awake, brother."

Brett. His rushed speech held a panicked note. Thankfully he was outside when it all went down. His shouts faded to the background as Alyssa's image grew blurry.

Just before the darkness closed in, her lips mouthed the words *I love you*.

Love you too, baby.

Always.

CHAPTER NINETEEN

"Should I open that other pint of ice cream or should I have a second brownie?" Lyss asked as she swung her legs over the edge of the couch. "Decisions, Decisions."

From her spot in a plush oversized armchair, legs dangling over one arm, Roxie tilted her head back and looked at Lyss. "Uh, did you really just ask that, chickie? Clearly, the answer is both. And while you're up, you can get me some more as well." She extended her arms in Lyss's direction, clanking her spoon against the side of an empty glass bowl.

"Huh, look how well that worked out for you," Lyss said.

"I know." Roxie winked and blew a kiss. "Love you."

"You better." Lyss grabbed her own bowl as well as her water glass and padded to the kitchen in her woolly socks. "Hold on, I'll grab your dishes in a minute. I can't be trusted to carry more breakables than I already have in my hands."

"Don't make me wait too long. You know mama gets mad if she has to wait too long for her chocolate."

With a chuckle, Lyss deposited her bowl and glass on the kitchen counter, then headed back to the den for Roxie's. "Hand it over."

Roxie gave her the dish then snatched the remote off the coffee table. "Mind if I flip on the local news? I want to check the scores."

"Go for it," Lyss said as she went back into the kitchen. After dropping a brownie in the bottom of Roxie's bowl, she opened the pint of Ben and Jerry's Half Baked and ladled a generous scoop on top.

"I totally forgot they were playing tonight. How are things with you and Gregg? I sorta got the impression when we talked the other day that things weren't all roses and sunshine," she called from the kitchen.

Roxie's boyfriend of about a year coached for Georgetown's football team. Seemed like a pretty good guy, though he hadn't spent too much time with Roxie's friends. In the fall especially, he was crazy with traveling and the team's rigorous training schedule.

"Rox?" Lyss called out. She squirted a stream of chocolate syrup into the bowl. Might as well go all out. There was a chance she was pregnant after all. That called for a serious chocolate binge.

"Oh, sorry. He's fine. Things are fine."

Fine. Hmm. Lyss had been a girl long enough to know fine was never fine. When she returned to the living room, it was to find Roxie frowning at the TV screen. Her spine was straight as an arrow and a glimmer of unease shone from her eyes. "They lost," she said, her voice flat.

"Oh, that's too bad." This was the first time Lyss had ever seen Roxie react this way. She had an almost…fearful look to her. Gregg's team had lost games before and Roxie always shook it off with a, *there'll be other wins.* Maybe things weren't so smooth sailing with her and her man. "Everything good, Rox? Gregg having a rough season?"

"Huh? What?" Roxie turned to Alyssa and blinked as though trying to get with the program. "Sorry, what did you say?"

"Just wondering if Gregg's team is having a bad season and if it's affecting your relationship. You seem…uneasy."

"Oh, yeah, sorry. They are having a craptastic season actually." She waved away Alyssa's concern and reached for her treat. "But we're fine. I'm just being dramatic. Besides, we're not here to talk about my love life. We're here to get sugared up because of your dumb husband."

"Ugh." She plopped down on the couch as the evening took a turn for the morose. "You had to bring it up, huh? I'd almost forgotten for about six seconds there."

With a snort, Roxie stuffed a giant spoonful into her mouth. "No, you hadn't," she said around her dessert.

No. She hadn't. Derek had been on her mind every second of the past few days. So much so, Hannah had forced her to go home from work midday. She'd mixed up a window treatment order, returned a call to the wrong client, and dropped a box of paint samples all over the floor. And that was just in the first hour. By noon, Hannah was so tired of putting out fires, she'd shooed Alyssa out the door with orders not to come back until she and Derek talked then had "all kinds of makeup sex."

About ten times that afternoon, she'd picked up her phone to call Derek then chickened out. He was going through something and needed time to work it out in his mind. Throughout the day, she ran through the gamut of emotions regarding to her husband.

First, she was pissed. Who the hell did he think he was to walk away after she'd dropped the bomb of a possible pregnancy? Then came the guilt. He was struggling, and she needed to support him. And back to anger. Support him? Um, hello? She could use some support as well. In the end, she'd called Roxie who showed up for an impromptu girls' night. Nothing like chocolate to soothe a battered heart.

Though hours in bed with her husband would have been preferred.

"He's not dumb, Rox. He's just acting dumb."

A very unladylike snort came from Roxie's chair.

"He's just finally processing everything that's happened and it's hitting him hard." She'd kept the antibiotic vs birth control contest quiet, not quite ready to talk about it. Every time she thought about bringing it up, her stomach took a nose dive.

Roxie grasped Alyssa's hand. "I know, hon. And that's fine. But he's pushing you away in the process. That's the dumb part."

With a sigh, Alyssa nodded. "I know. I'm ninety percent sure he's going to come to his senses in the next day or two and come home, but that ten percent that's convinced he's never coming back to me? Yeah that ten percent is a nasty bitch."

"Did you just say nasty bitch?" Roxie's mouth formed a dramatic O. She looked like the startled emoji. "Damn, girl. That's some serious language for you."

"Ha, ha. Aren't you supposed to be helping me, not mocking me?"

Back to her playful self, Roxie laughed. "Sorry, chickie. Hey, is there a reason I'm the only one eating here?"

"Oh!" Alyssa popped up. "Got all distracted with real-life nonsense. Let me get my food."

Worrisome thoughts invaded Alyssa's mind. In the kitchen, she propped her hands on the counter and bowed her head, taking a minute to collect herself. Derek would come home soon. He had to. Alyssa wasn't sure she could make her way through the rest of her life without him. They were a tight team. Or at least they used to be.

He'd be back.

She straightened and snatched the last brownie. After Derek was home and they put this chapter of their lives behind them, she'd revisit Roxie's relationship. Because there was something amiss there. Something Rox was troubled by. And since Alyssa loved Rox, second only to Derek, she'd figure out what it was and a way to help.

Just as she settled a brownie in the bottom of her bowl, a gasp came from the living room.

"Alyssa?" Roxie's voice trembled. "You need to get in here, now."

She frowned and grabbed her bowl before heading back to the living room. Maybe Roxie was ready to talk about whatever was bothering her. "What's u—"

She stopped dead in her tracks at the sight of her husband's face on the television screen. "What the…"

Roxie stood, her face pale and eyes wide, gaping at the screen. "Lyss," she said.

"We're coming to you live outside a convenience store in Adam's Morgan where reports of a robbery with shots fired are being investigated." A male reporter's voice blared through the TV. "We don't have much information at this point, but what we do know is that the man pictured here, Derek Jackson, a former SEAL and owner of the tattoo shop Trident Ink, just down the block from the convenience store, was shot while trying to disarm the robber."

A scream ripped from her throat and her legs crumpled. The glass bowl slipped through boneless fingers. It crashed to the wood floor and shattered in a thousand shimmery shards.

"Lyss!" Roxie cried, catching her just as she was about to hit the ground.

"Oh my God, Roxie," she said as a sob tightened her chest. "I can't…oh my God I can't lose him, too." Tremors wracked her body. The room was suddenly freezing, and she could barely think past the intense pain in her stomach and chest.

"Sweetie, breathe. They said he's alive and has been taken to the hospital."

"W-what?" Alyssa's breath hitched. Her chest felt so tight she could barely suck in air.

"The reporter said he was taken to the hospital."

"He-he's alive?" She forced her knees to straighten and keep her upright. "Which hospital?" She grabbed her friend's shoulders. "Which one, Rox?"

"I don't know, honey."

"We have to go. We have to find him. What hospital? Oh God. I can't drive. I'm shaking too much. You had some wine. Can you drive or have you had too much?"

Suddenly Ginuwine's *Pony* rang out through Alyssa's phone. "Brett," she said. "It's Brett." He'd set the ridiculous ringtone after Magic Mike premiered and he'd bragged that he was both a better dancer and better looking than Channing Tatum.

Alyssa scrambled over to the couch, her heart in her throat and her head full of worst case scenarios. By some miracle, she managed to avoid the glass all over the floor. Her hands shook so bad it took her three tries to swipe the phone open. "Brett? Have you seen the news?"

"He's alive, Lyss. I was there."

Her legs went limp again and she collapsed on the couch. Yes, the reporter had stated Derek was alive, but hearing it from Brett finally loosened the knot in her stomach. "Where are they taking him?"

"Washington Hospital Center, sweetie." Brett's voice was low, anxious.

"What happened? How bad is it?" She held the phone so tight in her grip she was afraid she'd crack the screen. But her fingers wouldn't loosen. The cell was her lifeline, her only link to information about her husband.

A sad chuckle left Brett. "You know our boy, Lyss. He's a born fuckin' hero. There was a robbery in the store while he was buying something. No way would he not try to intervene. He was seconds away from taking out the robber when another person in the store accidentally alerted the gunman to his presence. He was shot. After that the robber freaked and ran out of the store without any of the money. No one else was hurt."

Her chin dropped to her chest and tears fell from her eyes. "How bad?" she whispered.

Brett's swallow was audible. "Not sure, sweetie. They wouldn't let me ride with him. I'm about ten minutes out from the hospital. Do you need a lift? I can come get you."

"No. Go to him. I don't want him alone. Rox is with me. We'll leave right now.

"Okay, sweetie. He's one tough bastard and he loves you so much, Lyss. He won't leave you this way."

She sobbed out an okay, then disconnected the call.

"Washington Hos—"

"I could hear him. Uber's on the way. Three minutes out. Here." Roxie handed Alyssa her shoes and coat. "Let's go."

Thank God for Roxie. Alyssa probably would have run out into the thirty-five-degree night in fuzzy slippers and without a coat. Not to mention Uber hadn't even crossed her mind. Driving would be impossible. She was so freaked out she would be a hazard behind the wheel.

As though on autopilot, she stuffed her feet in her sneakers and arms in the coat. Normally she wouldn't be caught dead in her worn out Navy sweatpants and Derek's mammoth T-shirt, but this was so far from normal, nothing else mattered but getting to Derek.

"Come on, Lyss." Roxie guided her out the door and to the car waiting in the driveway.

"Washington Hospital Center, right?" the twenty-something female driver asked.

"That's right," Roxie said. "Emergency entrance."

"Gotcha." The driver shot Alyssa a curious look in the rearview mirror, but kept her curiosity to herself.

There was no better friend than Roxie, who laced her fingers with Alyssa's and held her hand. She didn't speak. Didn't try to make small talk or assure Alyssa all would be well. Because the words would be empty. Neither of them had any clue how the night would play out.

Alyssa stared unseeing out the window as they traveled into the city.

She'd already suffered a devastating loss in her life. Another one couldn't possibly be in the cards for her, could it?

If Derek died, she'd be left with nothing. No one. She had no family, well none that would accept her, and she wouldn't go to them anyway. There was Roxie, her sister in all but blood. She'd given Roxie a lot of herself over the years, but not everything. Derek was the only one who'd gotten everything, every little piece of her heart, mind, body, and soul. The only one who would ever get all of her. All her hopes, fears, desires, dreams.

If he died, she'd live out the rest of her life without giving those pieces to anyone ever again. She knew it deep in her bones. She just loved him that much. There just wasn't enough space in her heart to let another man in.

"Don't," Roxie said, squeezing her hand. "Just don't. We'll be there in a few minutes and we'll find out."

Tears streamed down her face as she swallowed. "I know."

After another ten minutes, the car came to a halt outside the glaring neon emergency sign at Washington Hospital Center in DC.

"I'm not sure I can get out," she whispered to Roxie.

Roxie gave her a stern look. "You can, chickie. Your man is waiting for you in there. And I can guarantee he's going to be a royal ass pain of a patient until you get in there and work your magic on him. In a non-sexual way, of course. Save the sexual healing until after he's discharged."

A ghost of a smile tipped Alyssa's lips. Rox was right. Derek hated to be sick or injured. Saw it as a sign of weakness, and he turned into a growly bear until he felt better.

She could do this. She could get out of the car, walk in the building, and inquire about her husband. She could hear the news—good news or bad. She had to. For him.

Then, she could wrap her arms around him and tell him how much she loved him.

Right before she blasted him for putting himself in danger.

As long as he was still alive.

CHAPTER TWENTY

Alyssa raced down the hallway of the emergency room like the hounds of hell were chasing her. Her unzipped jacket flapped back and forth as her feet pounded the tile floor.

"Two, four..." she mumbled as she streaked past the triage rooms. The moment the bored-looking receptionist informed her Derek was in room eight, Alyssa took off like she'd fired a starting gun in a race, leaving Brett and Roxie in the dust.

She didn't care. They'd catch up eventually. Her single-minded focus on seeing Derek alive was the only thing that mattered.

"Eight!" she cried as she wrenched the curtain open. Each triage room was separated by actual walls, but only a curtain closed the space off from the hallway.

And there he was. Sitting on a plint, shirt off, pale with dark circles under his eyes, and a bulky bandage over his left deltoid.

"Derek," she half spoke, half sobbed.

"Hey, baby." A wry grin lifted his lips and gave his tired face a teasing expression.

She scanned him, taking in every inch, looking for more injuries or signs something greater was wrong. All she saw aside from the shoulder injury was rounded muscles, a broad chest, and yards of colorful ink. Her eyes might have lingered for a second or two too long before returning to his face. It was easy to get lost in all that male perfection.

Especially when it was all for her and only her to enjoy. At least it had been all hers. The trauma of the night eclipsed all her previous worries and relationship concerns. Now that she could see for herself that Derek was alive and mostly unharmed, those anxieties began to come back.

Despite how glad she was to be there, their marriage was still like an overfilled balloon. For the past couple days, it felt as though at any second the entire thing would explode.

"Ahh, you must be Mrs. Jackson," a woman said from the corner of the room, making Alyssa jump. She'd been so zeroed on Derek, she hadn't noticed the short, curvy nurse in bright teal scrubs scanning medication packets with a handheld scanner attached to the wall computer.

"Um, yes, Alyssa," she replied. "How is he?"

"I'm fine," Derek said in the typical macho way he had. Once, a few years ago, he'd had a cough that was "fine" and remained fine for weeks on end while he got sicker and sicker, until Alyssa finally forced him to see his physician. Turned out to be a severe case of pneumonia, which landed him right in this very hospital for three days.

Stubborn alpha man.

"I didn't ask you, Der, I asked your nurse."

The nurse chuckled and shifted her long red braid, so it hung over her right shoulder. "I'm Nancy and I've been Derek's nurse since he was brought in here. For the most part he's right, he's fine, or at least he will be."

Derek smirked at him and she resisted the urge to stick her tongue out at the infuriating man.

"The bullet wound is just a deep graze that looks much more impressive than it really is. He didn't even loose much blood. We cleaned it and stitched him up. That arm will be sore for a few days and he'll probably have a scar, but that's the worst of it."

"Oh thank God," Alyssa said. "Can he leave tonight?"

"Well, we're going to keep him overnight."

Alyssa's eyes flew to Derek's. He didn't look remotely concerned, but then it could just be that macho bull crap again. "Overnight? How come?"

"He lost consciousness at the scene, which is what really had paramedics concerned. Luckily, he wasn't out for more than a few minutes, and he has a mild concussion. We'd like to keep him for one night, just to observe, and if all goes well he'll be released late morning."

"It's ridiculous. I'm fine. I barely even have a headache." Derek scowled at the nurse, who just raised an eyebrow.

"Nice try, Mr. Jackson, but I've been working here for fifteen years. Takes a lot more than a growl and a frown to intimidate me."

Despite the tears of relief that filled Alyssa's eyes, she chuckled. "You'll do exactly what they tell you or you'll answer to me."

The half smile he sent her was sad.

For a moment, they seemed so much like their old selves. The back and forth so familiar and comforting. But nothing was fixed. This was just a momentary break from the strain.

"Here's some pain medication, Mr. Jackson." Nancy handed him a small cup with three pills. "There's also an antibiotic in there."

After Derek swallowed the pills, the nurse nodded at him. "If there isn't anything else you need, I'll leave you two alone and see about getting you admitted to a room for the night."

"Thank you," Derek said.

As soon as she stepped out and closed the curtain the tension in the room thickened. Alone with Derek for the first time since she'd let him know her birth control might be ineffective, and he'd walked out, Alyssa had no idea how to act. No clue what to say.

The combination of intense relief that he wasn't severely injured combined with lingering adrenaline from those long moments not knowing if he was okay and the uncertainty of their status had her head spinning and tears leaking from her eyes.

All she wanted was to run to him, burrow into his warmth and strength and just erase the past few weeks. Well, the past couple years if she was really asking for a do over.

Instead, she just stood there with her arms lip at her sides, and tears streaming down her face. Despite being only three feet away from the man she loved more than anything in the world, she'd never felt more alone.

A bullet wound was nothing compared to the sight of Alyssa's tears. Combined with the horrible feeling of tension in the room and all he wanted to do was scoop her up, run home, and never let her leave his arms.

But that wouldn't solve anything. It would be a Band-Aid on a blast injury. With nothing but a curtain separating them from the rest of the hospital as well as some powerful pain pills beginning to course through his system, this was neither the time nor the place to delve into their issues.

So that left them staring at each other not having a clue how to proceed. He might as well just say what was in the front of his mind.

"I want to come home. To the house. When they discharge me."

Her mouth opened then closed then opened again. "Okay," she said. His poor wife looked about as frazzled as he'd ever seen her. Strands of long blond hair had slipped out of her messy bun and hung around her face. Some of her eye makeup had run and rimmed her eyes, giving her a racoonish appearance he'd never admit to noticing. Her jacket hung off one shoulder and she appeared to be wearing his giant shirt, sweats, and some fancy ankle boot things.

He couldn't have imagined a more beautiful woman. He should have told her, but it was as though he'd forgotten how to talk to her, how to connect.

She might be pregnant.

Standing there in front of him in that moment she might very well be carrying their child. Last time he'd thought of it, panic had tripped his throat like it was trying to strangle him. Now, he felt a flicker of excitement.

A baby.

They'd always wanted more kids, it just hadn't happened and then...

Well then life dealt them the worst hand possible.

It was at that moment, staring at each other with so much unsaid, so much grief, sorrow, guilt, and uncertainty standing between them, that the curtain slid open. A scowling Roxie stood rigid with her arms folded over her chest and Brett's arm slung over her shoulders.

He wore a shit-eating grin and his eyes twinkled with his typical mirth. If history was telling, Brett probably spent the last fifteen minutes working poor Roxie into a frenzy. There were some serious sparks between those two. Derek could never figure out why they hadn't ever hooked up. Instead of letting those sparks ignite into passion, they chose to burn each other with snarky remarks and insults.

It had to be some kind of long, drawn-out foreplay. Waste of time if you asked him, but to each his own.

"You know, man, if you'd just told me how much of a problem you had with the butterfly tattoo, I'd have cancelled my date. You didn't have to go and get shot to keep me from the lovely Jessica."

Derek grunted. "It wasn't a date and you damn well know it."

"Huh?" Lyss looked between the two men with a raised eyebrow. "What did we miss?"

"Sounds like Brett was on his way to a sleazy booty call when Der got shot. Surprise, surprise," Roxie said, her voice rife with disgust.

"Jealous, honey? You know if you ask real nice I just might throw you a—"

"Okay, Brett, we all get it. You're a stud. Now, leave Rox alone." Lyss had crossed the room and now stood with her arm around a frowning Roxie's shoulders. The stiffness in her posture relaxed when their friends joined them, like she needed some kind of buffer to feel comfortable around him.

That couldn't be a good sign.

They stayed and shot the shit for about forty-five minutes. Most of that time was him recounting the robbery for Lyss and Roxie. Where Roxie was fascinated with the story and rapid fired questions at him, Lyss drew in on herself the longer the story went on.

Maybe he shouldn't have described it in such detail. She'd had quite the scare that night. He tried to put himself in her shoes and it wasn't exactly a fun place to be. Had he heard Lyss was shot and didn't have any further information he'd have gone out of his fucking mind. He'd have torn the city apart to get to her and make sure she was okay.

After a while, Nancy returned to prepare him to be transported from the ER to a room for the rest of the night. He'd convinced Alyssa to go home and get some sleep. Brett lived a stone's throw from the hospital and offered to pick Derek up at discharge and drive him out to their home in Arlington.

Roxie and Brett begged out saying they'd give Lyss and Derek a few moments alone.

Great. A few more moments of awkward.

"Well, I guess I'll see you at the house tomorrow then."

It hurt. It physically hurt to see the aloofness in his normally warm and loving wife. He had no one to blame but himself for that one. But he planned to take the first steps toward mending the damage the second he stepped foot into his house.

"I'll be there. We'll talk," he said.

She held his gaze for a moment before flicking her attention to his shoulder. Then in a move he wasn't expecting, she rushed forward and gave him a gentle hug while planting a soft kiss on his cheek. "Thank you for being okay," she whispered against his ear. Then she stepped back and gave him another of those sad smiles before slipping around the curtain.

Alone with nothing to distract himself, two things happened. First, the pain in both the base of his skull and his shoulder screamed to life and made him groan out loud. And second, his mind went straight to thoughts of his troubles with Lyss.

Lyss said something to the therapist the other day. Something he hadn't understood at the time, but it was beginning to make sense now. She'd said life was moving forward whether they wanted it to or not. Whether they were lost in the past or not.

The world kept turning, the sun rose three hundred and sixty-five times per year, he aged, new clients discovered his business, and his wife was possibly pregnant.

Life moving forward.

There was a strange feeling forming in the pit of his stomach. Almost a flutter of, dare he say…excitement? Just a day ago he wouldn't have thought it possible, but seeing Alyssa burst in there tonight all disheveled and in a tizzy, potentially carrying his child, he didn't feel the abject panic that he had the other night.

Derek wasn't overly religious. He'd seen enough evil in the world to make him question the notion of a benevolent God. The jury was still out on whether or not he believed in an afterlife, but for some reason, he could almost feel Katie nudging him back into life.

Maybe that's what this was, whether a false alarm or a true pregnancy, maybe it was Katie's way of stepping in and giving him the push he needed. Because let's face it, he wasn't going to abandon Alyssa if she was having his child. Hell, he'd never leave her anyway, but they were stuck. They needed something to jolt the life back into their relationship.

"This your doing, Katie bug?" he whispered into the quiet room.

There wasn't an answer of course, but a sense of peace settled over him. That was answer enough.

Life moving forward.

CHAPTER TWENTY-ONE

Alyssa wiped invisible dust off the perfectly clean coffee table in her family room for the tenth time that morning. It was either that or vacuum again, and the idea of dragging the bulky machine down from her bedroom only to run it over a carpet she'd vacuumed just an hour ago wasn't very appealing.

"Argh!" She gripped her hair in frustration. She had to chill out. It was Derek, for crying out loud. He wouldn't give a flying fig if there was dust on the shelves or dirt in the carpet.

It was time to put down the duster and relax until Derek came home, which should be in the next half hour or so.

So, with chilling out in mind, Alyssa sank onto the plush couch, propped her bare feet on the coffee table she'd just re-dusted, and rested her head back. Sleep had been elusive, and she'd spent what little of the night remained after the hospital staring at the ceiling and planning what she wanted to say to Derek.

This reunion was going to go one of two ways. Either they were going to agree to come together, work toward fixing their issues, or it could potentially be the end of her marriage. She groaned as her stomach rolled with nausea. It was her worst nightmare, but as she'd heard time and time again, the death of a child so frequently led to the death of the marriage. It was just so damn difficult for two people who handled such a devastating emotional event in different ways to remain together. That sorrow remained between them forever growing and festering until the wound was gangrenous. And what happened to a non-healing infected limb?

It was amputated.

She did not want to be amputated from Derek's life.

But what if being with her meant continued suffering? What if he couldn't find a way to both be with her and learn to live with the anguish of Katie's death? Because that's how they had to deal with it. They'd never get past it, or move on from it. It was just learning to live with the reality of that horrific loss.

But for many, that didn't happen, if what she read was true. Add to it his misplaced guilt, and maybe being with her was just too damn painful for him.

In that case, she would let him go.

Despite what it would do to her, how it would completely destroy what remained of her already battered heart. She loved him that much and would do anything for him no matter the cost.

The thought made her physically ill. When she thought of a future without him, nothing came. Just blankness. He was so vital to her existence, and before Katie's illness she'd have said the same about her role in his life.

But she would do what she must to ensure Derek had a chance at happiness.

She blew out a breath and let her eyes drift closed. A few minutes of rest would do wonders for her raw nerves. The sleepless night sure hadn't helped anything.

"Lyss? Alyssa? Baby, wake up."

"What? Huh?" Alyssa dropped her feet and shot straight up as her heart pounded out of her chest. "Derek? Oh crap. I'm so sorry, I didn't mean to fall asleep for more than a few minutes. What time is it? When did you get back? How's your shoulder? Can I—"

Derek chuckled and plopped onto the couch to the left of her, his uninjured shoulder butting up against her. "Calm down,

Lyss. That's some serious rambling. I just walked in. My shoulder is fine, and I'm glad you're sleeping. I'm guessing you didn't get much last night."

"Maybe about ten minutes," she said as she flopped against the back of the couch. She turned her head and found Derek gazing at her, a mixture of heat and sadness in his eyes. "I can't do this anymore. This thing where we tiptoe around each other like we've forgotten who we are, so I'm just going to rip of the Band-Aid and tell you what I obsessed about all night. Really for the past few months, but I think I figured it out in my head last night."

With a nod, Derek linked his fingers with hers and held tight. "Okay."

It took a moment to gather the strength to speak, and after a hard swallow she said words she never could have imagined would cross her lips. "I do not want to be what keeps you from finding peace and happiness again in life."

The look of shock that crossed his face was almost comical despite the heaviness of the situation. When he opened his mouth, she held up her hand. "Just let me say it all, okay?"

He nodded, but the tick in his jaw told her he wasn't happy about it.

"Looking at me has to be a constant reminder of what we lost. Of whatever guilt—although totally misguided—that you're feeling. And now I've dropped the bomb of a possible pregnancy when the idea of it is terrifying. I want to give..." She almost couldn't say the words. "I want to give you an out," she said, stronger this time.

"Lyss," he said, shaking his head. His voice was so weighed down with pain.

"If you need to be away from me, either temporarily or permanently, I'll understand. Knowing you stayed with me and let yourself be eaten alive by guilt and pain would be so much worse than knowing you left, but were able to live a life with some contentment again." She choked out the last words and swiped at the tears that wouldn't remain in her eyes with an almost violent smack.

Inside, her stomach twisted and turned until she felt the knots would never come undone and her heart ached with an unfathomable pain. She had to sink her teeth into her bottom lip to keep her mouth from opening and screaming how it was all a lie and begging him to stay with her.

But she couldn't do that to the man she loved. Couldn't condemn him to a life of heartache.

"Jesus, Lyss." He dropped her hand and bent forward, elbows on his knees. Instead of speaking right away, he linked his hands behind his head and she would have sworn she heard a small sniff. After what felt like an hour, but was probably only ten seconds, he lifted his head and she was shocked to her core to see a sheen of wetness in his eyes.

"Living one more second away from you is the last fucking thing I want, Lyss."

Oh thank God.

Relief hit her so hard she felt weak and drained.

"I'm never going to be without you again, Lyss. Can I say a few things now?" He faced her, grabbed one of her hands, and brought the palm to his lips.

She leaned forward as his lips brushed her skin and rested her forehead on his uninjured shoulder. "Yes," she whispered. "Go ahead."

Warmth spread through her just from the innocent contact of her head on him and her hand in his. The road moving forward wouldn't be easy, but at least she didn't have to do it alone.

Alyssa's words had been like a smack in the face. If he hadn't been sitting right next to her listening as they left her mouth, Derek never would have believed what she was saying. She didn't want to live without him, of that he was one hundred percent certain, yet she was willing to forego her own happiness to give him what she thought he needed.

Good thing she was so fucking far from knowing what he needed in that moment. Because there was only one thing he needed then and only one thing he'd need for the rest of his damn life.

And that was her.

Lyss.

His beautiful, selfless, loving wife.

He gently nudged her off his shoulder and looked straight into her ocean-blue eyes. Suddenly it all seemed easier. Natural. Like he couldn't wait to get the words out of his mouth. Words that would help mend the fissures in their relationship.

"Being with you the past few times, touching you, tasting you, being inside you, was exactly what I needed to remind me of what I was missing. And pretending to be someone else gave me the freedom to enjoy it, enjoy you, without the heavy baggage of the past couple years sitting between us."

"It was the same for me, Der. I wanted so many times over the past year to try to get us back to where we were, but I couldn't figure out how to get there with so much sadness between us. It was like there was a giant fissure between us and neither of us could find a way over or around it. You could practically taste the grief in our house, it was so thick."

"It was a good idea. Getting Maggie involved, trying her crazy plan."

"Well," she said as she squeezed his hand, "it seems like it was working until the end of the second…uh…encounter. Then it all went downhill, and you left. What happened?"

Derek tucked a wayward piece of hair behind her ear, leaving his hand cupped around the back of her neck. "Everything I'd been suppressing for so long came flooding in. You were there with me, all beautiful and satisfied and open to me. More than just physically. And I just realized how close I came to losing everything. I felt guilty, like I'd failed our marriage. From there it all just spiraled." He shrugged.

"Spiraled into what? Because you pushed me away instead of pulling me in."

"Yeah." Baring his soul sucked. "Being a protector, being proactive, attacking problems...it's what I was trained to do for so many years that it's now ingrained in me. It's in my blood. Who I am and all that shit. None of it stopped when I left the SEALS. It just changed. Now, instead of protecting and fighting for my country, I did that for my business, my friends, and most importantly for you, Lyss. And then Katie."

Would it ever get easier to say her name?

"There wasn't a damn thing we could have done beyond what we tried to save her. And the same could happen to you and I'd be just as powerless. It fucked with my head. Had me thinking I couldn't take care of you in other ways. Couldn't protect you. Which had me thinking you'd be better off without me."

"Derek, that's not—"

He lifted her soft hand to his mouth and kissed her palm. Her eyes went liquid. Two pools of deep blue he'd gladly drown in. "I know, baby. It's not true. It doesn't even really make sense. I was just in a bad head space. I'm not trying to make excuses for myself because it's wrong either way. Then you told me your birth control might have failed, and I went into full-on panic mode. I freaked out and walked away. And now you think I want out of our marriage. God, Lyss. I'm so fucking sorry."

Before he had a chance to say anything further, a firm but delicate hand covered his mouth. Did it make him a prick that his first instinct was to slide his tongue through the slit between her fingers and watch her eyes grow hazy with desire?

Maybe a little.

Thankfully, he'd honed enough self-control over the years to avoid the temptation.

Just barely.

"Stop," she said, a sympathetic smile tilting her lips. "Just stop. Whatever it is you feel the need to apologize for, whatever you think you screwed up, it's forgiven. What I learned from the past few weeks is that there isn't a script for handling something like our daughter d-dying."

An invisible fist squeezed his heart at Lyss's fumble. Seeing her struggle through the emotions was even worse than being in pain himself.

"You're here now. And I'm here now. That's what matters." She sniffed, and tears leaked from her eyes. "I was so afraid it was over."

And therein lay his guilt. That he allowed her to feel that way. That he *made* her feel that way because he was too fucked up to handle things properly.

"And I know that's what you feel bad about. But don't. Please. I'm asking you to let go of the guilt. We have enough legitimate hurt and sorrow to deal with. We don't need to create any more."

Her eyes were watery with faint purple smudges under them. A memento from the previous sleepless night. When they were done, he was going to make sure she slept for a week. After he got his fill of her, of course.

Her words touched somewhere deep in him, putting a bandage over the bleeding wound that had been festering for too long. He couldn't wait any longer. With the hand wrapped around the back of her neck, he hauled her against him, kissing her with all the love and gratitude he felt.

And it was a fuckload.

She stiffened for a nanosecond then melted against him.

Before releasing her, he whispered against her ear. "I'm the luckiest bastard out there."

She gave him a small smile, but the tears were gone, replaced with heat and promise.

They talked for what had to be hours. Lyss really opened up about her internal war between wanting to be a mother again and the deep-seated fear of something happening to any children they might have. If there was some way he could ease her mind, guarantee any children they had would live long happy lives, he'd do it in a heartbeat.

Pay any amount of money.

Break any laws necessary.

Sacrifice any body part.

But as they found out the very hard way, life didn't work like that. There were no guarantees.

They'd both agreed to continue their sessions with Maggie. Neither was under the illusion that this talk today would erase two years of distance and drifting. But it was an enormous step in the right direction and for the first time in longer than he could remember, Derek felt some peace in his soul.

After a while exhaustion crept over him and his shoulder began to throb to a powerful beat. By that time, he was sprawled out on the couch with Lyss tucked into his non-injured side and he'd be damned if he disturbed her by going to get some pain medication. He'd had worse and would tough it out with ease.

"We should get up," Lyss said after they'd been silent for a few moments.

"We will, babe. We're both exhausted. Close your eyes."

She wrapped her arm around his waist and gave a gentle squeeze. "Love you, Derek," she said, her voice already drowsy with impending sleep.

"Love you too, Lyss."

CHAPTER TWENTY-TWO

Warmth was the first sensation that registered. Then a feeling of safety and rightness. Alyssa blinked, trying to clear the cobwebs. She was lying curled up half on Derek and half on their couch.

Derek was home. The sweetest words she'd ever thought.

She blinked and gazed around her family room. Darkness blanketed the room but for the glow of the neon clock on the blue ray player. Nine at night. They'd been asleep for hours, both needing the rest after such an emotionally draining few weeks.

Slowly, so as not to wake her sleeping husband, Alyssa wormed out of his hold and off the couch. Really, it was a fairly easy task as Derek slept like the dead when fully relaxed. It had taken him ages to be able to do that, plagued by nightmares and years of training to be somehow both asleep and alert while in the military.

Now, he looked so peaceful in his slumber. Still handsome as ever. From the very first time she'd laid eyes on him, he took her breath away. Tall, strong, powerful, commanding. A shiver raced through her. He was all those things and more, both in and out of their bedroom.

While sleeping all wrapped up in Derek arms was heaven, sleeping on that couch with a man his size wasn't exactly like sleeping on a cloud. She rolled her neck across her shoulders and winced at sharp crick in her neck.

A steaming hot shower and two ibuprofens should do the trick. Part of her wanted to wake Derek and entice him to join her in the shower. Conserving water was one of her all-time favorite activities.

Between Derek being injured and the pressure cooker of the past few weeks, she was beyond ready for a release or two.

Or four or five, knowing her husband.

Hearing her strong husband express his pain, guilt, and feelings of inadequacy actually hurt her heart. Then delving into her fear of becoming a mother again. Heavy stuff for the day after Derek was shot. She felt like she'd taken a beating and she wasn't even the one who was shot and concussed.

No, she'd let him sleep for now. Plenty of time to play later.

They had their whole lives.

All her life, Alyssa wanted to be a mother. She was raised in a very strict, conservative, manner, where woman stayed in the home, raised children, kept house, and served their husbands. There were no choices, no other options, no balance between career and family. Women had one role and one role only, homemakers. It wasn't being a homemaker she'd had a problem with. Not at all. It was the lack of choices. Lack of free will.

Difficult way for someone like her to grow up. Someone who had a love of design and colors, and making things not only beautiful, but meaningful, personalized. Not only did her parents strongly disapprove of her desire to become an interior designer because it would take away from her obligations to her family and father's church community, but they also accused her of being materialistic. Seduced by worldly desires.

It had been a serious struggle, but with Derek's support, she'd broken away from that life and found one where she could pursue her dreams.

That being said, the desire to be a mother had been instilled young and stuck around even when she didn't. And it was still there. The urge to raise a child, maybe more than one. But it was blanketed by a fear so powerful she wasn't sure she could overcome it. The notion of having another child that could be hurt terrified her. So much was out of her or Derek's control. So much could go horribly wrong.

As she made her way to the master bathroom, she rested her hand on her lower stomach. She very well could be pregnant right at that moment.

Instead of the stranglehold of panic and terror that had kicked every other time she contemplated that fact, this time she was hit with a sharp mental image of the future.

It was so clear, she'd swear it was real. Derek running around their back yard with a dark haired, squealing boy on his shoulders. Both had huge grins on their faces as they played.

Her steps faltered. Holy crap. That feeling? The fluttering in her stomach and zing in her blood? That was excitement.

She was excited about the prospect of having another child.

With a grin and a lighter step than she'd had in months, Alyssa entered the master bathroom. After turning the shower on full blast, she dug around for something to wear afterward. What she'd love to do was slip into some lingerie and seduce her husband, but considering the head injury and bullet wound, even Derek was likely to take a pass on lovemaking for the evening.

By the time she returned to the shower, the water had warmed and clouds of white steam hung thick in the bathroom. The instant the hot water rained down on her neck, her muscles relaxed. Took a few hours on the couch to knot it all up, but thirty seconds under the water, and she felt everything loosen.

She washed her hair and body with vanilla scented products —Derek's favorite—then shaved all the necessary areas until she was smooth and smelling pretty damned good. Lingering wasn't the wisest idea since he could wake at any time, but the heat of the water beating down on her was hypnotic.

Just a few more minutes then she'd get out

She closed her eyes and tilted her face into the stream, arching her back.

"If that's not the sexiest fucking thing I've ever seen, I don't know what is."

Alyssa gasped and righted herself. Derek's voice hit her the same time a waft of cold air cut through her steamy paradise. He stood in the open door of the glass shower, one arm over his head and leaning on the frame. Wearing nothing but some ink, a smile, and a lumpy bandage on his left shoulder, he stared at her with smoldering, hungry eyes. Between his legs, his thick cock jutted out, tempting her beyond reason.

"Derek," she said on a breath. She was sure he could see the love and desire shining in her eyes. There was no point in hiding it. After two years of heartache, struggle, loss, and pain, they'd found their way back to each other. For the rest of their lives, she'd make sure he knew just how loved and wanted he was.

He stepped into the shower and wrapped his solid arms around her, drawing her flush against her very favorite set of abs. If she'd thought the shower was warm, it was nothing compared to the heat radiating off her man. His was the kind of warmth that burrowed deep into her heart and soul, heating every cell in her body. Especially those between her legs.

"Wait, Derek, your shoulder," she said. "Are you allowed to get it wet? And you have a concussion. You should probably lie down some more."

"The bandage is waterproof. Doc said it was fine. That nap did wonders for my headache. Even if it wasn't all good, nothing is keeping me from my wife right now."

"But—"

"I missed you," he whispered as he dipped his head. His lips and breath tickled her ear, causing goosebumps to rise all over her skin despite the heat of the water. "I've missed you so damned much, Lyss."

Concern for his wound was replaced with need. "Me too, Derek. I—"

"Wait," he said pulling back until their gazes met. "You know I'm not the smoothest with the words, unless we're talking dirty words." He winked. "But I want to tell you something."

Alyssa nodded, and her heartrate kicked up. Despite what he thought, he could have her a quivering pile of need with just a few words. "Go ahead."

"There's no denying the past two years have been awful. We've talked, and will continue to talk to each other, and with Maggie, about Katie and our relationship, but I think we are both finally starting to heal in that regard. Not that the wound will ever fully close…"

He stared down at her like he was unsure of how to express himself and she gave him a soft smile. "I understand what you mean." And she did. They'd never forget Katie. Never stop grieving her loss. But they would get to the point where they could think about her with love and remember the wonderful times instead of feeling a gut-wrenching pain whenever her name was mentioned.

With a nod, Derek picked up one of her hands and held it over his heart. "I could always feel you here, and I haven't been able to feel you lately." His smile turned sad. "You're everything, Lyss. *Everything*. Whatever I do, wherever I am, I can always feel you," he said as he pressed her hand harder over his heart. "And it's slipped away so slowly I didn't realize how closed my heart was. And then all of a sudden, I was empty. You were here, but I couldn't feel you. And I miss you in there so goddamned much. My heart is open again. Please come back in, and I promise I'll lock you in there so tight, you'll never get out again."

Though she'd promised herself she was done with crying, tears mixed with the water running down her face. He'd just described so perfectly everything she'd been feeling but unable to put into words. Her own heart had hardened the day Katie died, unable to bear the pain and unwilling to allow the possibility of further pain. So it had closed.

"I will do anything to get back in, Derek." She choked out the words. "I'm here and I'm never going anywhere."

"Anything, huh?" he asked as his lips quirked. "Even hire some therapist with a crazy sex plan?" He released her hand and trailed his own up and down her spine.

"It worked, didn't it?" Her nipples stiffened to taut peaks as his hands roamed over her slick body.

A genuine laugh left him. "I think it's pretty safe to say a plan involving you naked and coming will work for damn near anything." His hands settled on her ass and pulled her against him, one leg on either side of his thick thigh. He ground her against the firm muscles until she gasped and let out a little moan. "Hope you said all you have to say, because we're done talking."

"Yeah, I'm good," she said. She could barely think, let alone talk as the course hairs and sculpted planes of his thigh rasped against her clit.

"Feel good?"

"Yes."

"You're wet, baby."

"We *are* in the shower."

"Not what I mean, and you know it, smartass. You want me?" his eyes were heavy lidded, and his hands flexed against her ass. Ten fingers holding her tight.

"God, yes. I'm dying here, Derek." In a move so fast, she never saw it coming, he spun her until her front was pressed against the shower wall. When her warm nipples hit the cooler tile, she yelped, and Derek chuckled.

His big body curled around hers from behind, engulfing her and making her feel small, feminine. One at a time, he lifted her hands and placed them on the slippery tile wall above her head then held them in place.

"You ready to feel even better?" With an excruciating slowness, he trailed the tips of his fingers from their joined hands, along the outside of her arm, over the curve of her breast, down the softness of her belly, and straight to her clit.

The many seconds it took him to get there, knowing that was his destination, were agonizing. She trembled, crowded between her husband and the wall as he circled her clit then moved on to tease the opening of her sex.

"Asked you a question, gorgeous," he said, dipping one finger into her then right back out again. Her pussy clenched, an effort to keep him inside, but he was too fast.

She whimpered. "Y-yes. Ready." Her head dropped forward, landing on the shower wall with a gentle thunk.

"Good girl," he said, slipping a long finger back in her pussy at the same time his teeth closed over the side of her neck. "You miss this? You miss me inside you? Fucking you with my fingers? My tongue?" As he spoke, he brushed his thumb over her clit and a second finger joined the one wreaking havoc inside her.

Then, the hard length of his erection pressed into the base of her spine. "My cock?" he asked.

Miss it? He had no clue. Not one freaking clue.

God yes, she'd missed the pleasure. The orgasms. Hers and watching his. But, just as much, she'd missed the connection. Knowing there was only one person in the world she shared this closeness with. Only one person who got her heart, mind, and body.

"Yes, I missed it, Derek," she said as his fingers sped up and his free hand palmed a breast. He worked her nipple, twisting and pinching with just the right amount of pressure. Just shy of too hard. The small bite of pain shot straight to her clit.

"Me too, baby. Me too. Nothing better than this hot pussy sucking me in. Any part of me. You want more?"

"I want everything."

"Damn, that's a good answer, baby." He pressed kisses along the back of her bent neck and down the first few inches of her spine.

When his two fingers slipped from her, she cried out in protest. "No!"

"Shh," he whispered against her ear. "Don't worry, baby. When have I not taken care of you? I'll give you what you need." He slid his thumb through her saturated folds, gathering the wetness. Then, he moved his thumb back, until it was pressed against the tight ring of her ass.

She tensed, but only for a second. They'd done plenty of anal play in the past, and she liked it. Really liked it. But the thin line between pleasure and pain always brought just a hint of anxiety along with it. That was a bit of a turn on in and of itself.

"You good?" He licked the shell of her ear and she had to fight to keep her eyes from rolling back in her head.

"So good. Just been a while."

"Too long."

"Yeah."

As he worked his thumb into her anus, he shoved two fingers back into her pussy and pinched her nipple with his other hand. The pleasure changed from a slow, burning build up to a sharp, almost harsh sensation.

"Oh God, Derek," she said on a moan as his thumb seated in her fully. He began to rock his hand back and forth alternating the deep penetration between his fingers in her pussy and his thumb in her ass.

The shower stall grew almost unbearably hot, her breath came in rapid hitches, and the world became hazy.

"Shit, baby, love the sound of my name when I'm fucking you. Say it again."

"Derek," she said. It wasn't her normal voice. It was a desperate, needy plea for release.

"That's fuckin' right. Know we've been playing games these past two weeks. And I love playing with you, but never again. You'll never call me another man's name again." His hand increased in speed and intensity until she was so lost in the sensations she could barely make sense of his words.

"I'll play whatever games you want to play. Be whatever you want me to be. The cable guy. A CEO. The fuckin' mail man. But you will only call me Derek. Especially when I'm fucking you. Especially when you're coming."

With that, his fingers moved at a furious pace. Her legs shook so hard, she was pretty sure the only thing holding her up was his hand between her legs. He left her breast and pinched her clit between his thumb and forefinger. "Say it now," he growled.

"Derek!" she screamed as her vision went white and her world consisted of nothing but pleasure. He kept at her through the orgasm until the quaking subsided and she slackened against him.

After removing his hand, he turned her around and gripped her head between his palms. He brought her mouth so close a breath couldn't squeeze between them.

"Am I dead?" she asked with a lazy smile. Pleasure chemicals coursed through her system. Her limbs were limp, heavy. For the first time in two years, she felt truly satisfied.

"Hope not," he whispered against her mouth. "We're just getting started."

That was exactly what she'd been hoping he'd say.

"Welcome home, Derek," she said as she snaked her arms around his neck and pressed her lips to his.

Finally, finally she could begin to move forward with her life.

Derek was home.

CHAPTER TWENTY-THREE

If Derek didn't get inside Alyssa in the next sixty seconds, there was a high chance he'd expire on the spot. Feeling her come on his fingers was close to heaven, but he needed her with a strength he hadn't experienced before. More than just physical, he needed to feel joined to her. Needed to renew the connection they both thrived on.

Once again, his shoulder was on fire, but there was no way in hell he'd be downing any pain medications until he was good and done fucking his wife. Nothing would be dulling any of the sensations he was about to experience.

Nothing.

He ended the kiss and stroked his hands all over her wet body. Her skin was soft and slick, and he couldn't get enough of just touching her. Feeling that she was really there, in his arms, about to be in their bed.

The water had cooled so he cut it off and reached for the towel she'd hung on a hook outside the shower. "Step out."

She complied immediately, and he rubbed the towel over her body. Even though she'd just come, there was a burning need reflected in her eyes. Her body twitched and shivered as he dried her, sensitive from the recent orgasm. "Get on the bed. On your back. Legs spread. I'll be there as soon as I dry off."

"Hurry," she said before turning and strolling to their neatly made king-size bed.

It was an effort to tear his gaze away from the smooth slope of her back and the curve of her ass, but his reward would be better than just a visual treat, so he dried as fast as possible and joined her in the bedroom.

As requested, she was on her back in the center of their bed. The dark purple comforter contrasted the golden hue of her saturated hair. She'd spread her legs, bent at the knees, and waited for him with a seductive smile.

Getting fully back on track wasn't something that would happen in the blink of an eye. A couple didn't go through two years of disconnect and bounce back in a mere week or two. And most likely, their relationship wouldn't be the same as it was before. Too much had happened. Too much sorrow. Too much sadness. But they could still be strong, hell, maybe even stronger for having trudged through the darkness and emerged in the light.

Yes, in that moment, staring at his wife laid out before him, Derek was one hundred percent confident they'd not only get back to where they'd been two years ago, but they'd be sturdier.

"How is it possible," he asked as he knelt on the end of the bed, "that you get sexier and sexier with each passing year?"

She tilted her head and straightened one leg, sliding her foot up his thigh. A laugh bubbled out of her. Fantastic sound that hadn't had much chance to be used lately. "Guess it's just my special gift to the world," she said with a roll of her eyes.

Didn't matter how often he told her, part of her never quite believed she was as stunning as he proclaimed. Silly woman.

Good thing he had the next forty plus years to convince her.

"The world?" He reached out and circled a delicate ankle with his hand.

"Not the world. Just you. Always just you."

"That's right baby." He stroked up the silky skin of her calf and over her knee to her thigh. "All this gorgeous, just for me. All this sweet, kind, intelligent…" He shook his head. It was his and he'd almost let it go.

"It's over now, Derek. We've found our way back. No more sadness. Just love me." She widened her legs further and scooted down the bed until her drenched sex pressed against his knees.

His dick rested atop his thighs pointing straight toward her tits. He'd love to come on them, see them decorated with the evidence of his desire for her. But it would have to hold until next time. Because there was only one place he'd be getting off right now, and that was deep in her tight pussy.

He grabbed her hands with his and bent forward, looming over her. He pressed their joined hands into the damp mattress beside her head. Then, he kissed her lips, her cheek, her chin. With a soft sigh, she tilted her head back giving him access to her neck. Answering her unspoken request, he continued kissing his way down the underside of her chin to her tits.

As he closed his mouth over her taut nipple, she arched her back. "Yess," she hissed. He sucked strongly on her nipple before releasing it and licking his way over to its twin. This time, he nipped the underside of her breast, causing her to yelp, then giggle.

She wasn't as full as she'd once been. Not quite as perky. Nursing Katie had done that to her, but he hadn't lost one bit of interest in her body post baby. In fact, the evidence of her having had a child, the widening in her hips, the softness of her belly was so innately feminine it only made him more attracted to her. The thought of her filling again, rounding out with another child had white-hot desire shooting through his veins.

Yeah, it was pretty safe to say he was getting on board with the idea of having another child.

Still holding her hands captive, he trailed his lips down her torso.

"Later," she said, as he was about to get his mouth on her sex. Her voice was strained with need. "I want to feel you inside me. No more playing. No more waiting."

Well, that certainly worked for him.

He rose to a tall kneel and released her hands before scooping under her knees and placing her calves on his shoulders. He was careful to avoid the bandages, but with all anticipation coursing through him, pain had all but disappeared.

Without being asked, she reached between his legs and circled his cock. Her hand closed in a firm grip and she stroked over the sensitive skin at the same time she tilted her hips and dragged the head of his cock through her soaked folds.

"Fuck." He dug his fingers into her thighs where they rested at his shoulder level. "So damn hot."

This time, when she slid him through her hot flesh, she halted at her opening and let go.

"You want my cock, baby?"

She nodded frantically.

There was something about seeing her spread out before him, legs wide, waiting for his cock. He wasn't a sadist by any means, but he enjoyed the flash of desperation in her eyes as he held back for a moment, making her wait, making her beg.

"Derek, please."

He needed no further prompting and thrust into her in one long, hard stroke.

"Yes," she cried out as her hips rose, aiding in the penetration.

This was it. This was everything. It went too far beyond the physical pleasure, to a soul-deep connection. She wanted. She needed. And he was the only man who would ever fulfill that need. The only man who would satisfy her sexually, but also with his love. Buried inside her, they were linked in every possible way and it was as vital to him as breathing.

The moment he bottomed out, he paused and just enjoyed the feel of her warm, tight grip on every inch of his shaft. Her eyes were at half mast, lips swollen from his kisses, hair a tangled wet mess around her head. She was breathtaking. "Tell me what you're feeling."

"Full," she answered at once. "Here." She clenched her pussy around him causing him to grunt and see stars. "And here." Her hand pressed over her heart.

There wasn't a better answer than that.

"Gonna fuck you now."

"About time." She winked and blew him a kiss.

With a snicker, he pulled out then slammed back into her, drawing a sharp cry of pleasure from her lips. That sound, the involuntary acknowledgement of how damn good she was feeling broke the last shred of his control.

He pounded into her again and again, soaking up each and every whimper, grunt, and moan she emitted.

This was where he belonged.

This was his home.

This was where he'd heal.

It didn't take more than a few minutes before his balls grew heavy and tight with the need for release. He gritted his teeth and tried to hold off, tried to make it last, but when Alyssa's cries grew frantic and she clawed at his back trying to pull him even tighter against her, he knew it was a battle he wouldn't win.

Bending forward, he folded her nearly in half and whispered against her ear. "Still love you, Lyss. Loved you every day of the last two years. Even if I didn't show it. Come with me now."

She turned her head and met his gaze. He thrust two more times, came with a force so powerful he almost wasn't able to keep his eyes open and watch Lyss come. Her mouth opened, and a harsh gasp flew out as her body went rigid beneath him. Ten sharp nails pricked into his back. He fucking loved that sensation. When she lost control enough to forget to be careful.

As though he'd shot all his energy out his dick, he slumped down on her. Their chests met then retreated with their rapid breathing. After a few minutes, Alyssa wiggled, and he realized he was still holding her legs up. Her knees were nearly at her ears. Poor thing probably felt crushed.

"Sorry, babe," he said, as he maneuvered his arms so her legs could drop to the bed.

Strong, slender arms looped around his back. "Don't completely go. I was just squished. I'm good now. I still want to feel your weight."

He shifted so he was only half lying on her, giving her enough space to breathe. He rested his head on her chest as her fingertips caressed up and down his sweat-dampened back. The other hand, he placed over her lower abdomen. "We didn't use a condom."

Her hand stilled. "I know. And I stopped taking the pill, just in case I was pregnant."

Her words surprised him. The honest truth was additional protection hadn't even crossed his mind. She was his wife and they hadn't had a need for condoms since before they were married. "You okay with that?"

The question was met with a silence that had a bit of nervousness skittering through him. "Lyss?" He popped his head up and watched her face.

"I think I am. For this time. I'm not ready to actively start trying, but if it happens…"

He smiled. "Yeah? Well, I'll pick up some condoms. If it turns out you're not pregnant, you can go back on the pill until we decide we are ready. I'm good either way. Okay?" It was the truth.

"Okay. I love you too, Derek. You know that, right? That hasn't wavered at all. Just like you said."

"Never doubted it for a second, Lyss." And he hadn't. This had never been about a lack of love. The whole fucking world could be crumbling around them and the one constant would be their love.

"Derek?" Her hand absently sifted through the hair at the base of his scalp.

"Yeah, babe?" He nuzzled the side of her breast with his nose. This moment was perfect. There wasn't one thing that could make it better.

"Let's have brunch here this Sunday."

He shifted so he was positioned over her once again, staring down at the sated and happy look on her face. They'd come full circle.

He was wrong, the moment could get better.

"You got it," he said as he claimed her mouth, ready to love on her all over again.

EPILOGUE

It was Sunday, brunch day. The second one since Derek's injury and their reconciliation.

And it was seven days after her period was due.

It came like clockwork. Never a day early. Never a day late. Until she'd gotten pregnant the first time around. And until today.

Her friends and chosen family milled around downstairs, eating, laughing, and completely unaware of the impending nervous breakdown one floor above them in the master bathroom. She should have waited, had tried to wait, but she sat at the table obsessing and needed to put herself out of her misery.

Earlier that morning, it had hit her like a lightning strike. Seven days. Seven days late. She'd been so busy with work and Derek, that the lack of period had gone unnoticed. Until today. The day when she was having a houseful of people for brunch. As they'd done every Sunday until Katie got sick and had recently started again.

So, under the guise of needing more orange juice, she'd gone to the store and purchased a pregnancy test. It had taken five minutes of staring at the shelf to get her hands to listen to her brain and actually pull the box from the shelf. Of course, they'd been trembling the whole time. This was a moment she'd been petrified of for the past few years.

After Derek came home, they'd sort of had an unspoken pact not to mention the possibility looming over them.

And now it may all be upon her.

As was the way of life, there'd been an accident that blocked her route home and she'd returned at the same moment Roxie showed up. Hunter, who was quickly becoming a close friend of the both her and Derek, arrived about thirty seconds later. She'd decided she could wait until the guests had left and she was alone.

But that hadn't worked. So now she was hiding out in her bathroom trying to stare at anything but the little stick waiting on the closed toilet lid.

Was she ready to be a mother again? It was the main issue she was working on in therapy with Maggie during her solo sessions. The times with Derek were spent focusing on their relationship, and the alone time for individual growth and healing.

Despite the progress she was making, lingering fears still had a solid grip on her. There were too many things that could go wrong. The potential for soul-crushing pain too high.

"Babe? Where you at?" Derek's voice rang out from their bedroom.

"In here," she called. "Just fixing my hair." It was a half-truth. She'd gotten warm cooking and needed a tie to hold her hair back.

Two seconds later, her husband's large form filled the doorway between their bedroom and bathroom. "Babe, is there something going on with Roxie? Has she seemed off to you lately?"

God, she loved this man. He cared about her friend's welfare just as much as she did. "Actually, I did notice. She's been strange for the past month. I think something is up with her and Gregg. I'm going to try to get together with her for lunch on Tuesday. I'll ask her about it then."

"Sounds good. You hiding out up here?" He strode into the room and she positioned herself so she was blocking his view of the toilet.

"No. Just needed a minute. I'll be right down."

He narrowed his eyes and folded his arms across his muscular chest. "Lyss? What's going on?"

He knew her too well. Like a bloodhound, he could always sniff out if she was having a problem. The alarm on her phone chimed. Three minutes were up. She swallowed.

"What's that?"

Her eyes locked with Derek's. It was as though her tongue thickened in her mouth, making speaking impossible. Her heart pounded as she stepped to the left, revealing the pregnancy test waiting on the toilet seat.

Derek's gaze shifted then returned to hers, this time wide eyed. "I—" His Adam's apple rose and fell as he swallowed. "Is it time to look?"

She nodded. No point in delaying it. With nausea rolling in her gut, she grabbed the test. It wobbled in her hands. Derek stepped forward and surrounded her shaking fingers with his strong, steady ones, lending his never-ending strength.

"Whatever it says, it'll be okay, Lyss. I promise."

She nodded and for the sake of her husband, pretended she had the strength for this. She gazed down at the test.

Two blue lines.

Pregnant.

Pregnant.

Joy hit her so hard she almost fell to her knees. Any worry, doubt, fear she'd been harboring disappeared the second her eyes caught that second line. She was going to be a mother again.

"It's positive," she said holding the stick in front of Derek's face. "Oh my God, it's positive."

Derek let out a tremendous whoop and lifted her off her feet, spinning her around. When he set her down, he cupped her face and kissed her. "Are you okay?"

"I...yes, I am. If you'd asked me yesterday I would have told you I was still terrified. But seeing it now in front of me. I'm good. More than good. I'm ecstatic."

Pregnant.

Derek couldn't believe it. Once he'd gotten over his initial poor reaction to the possibility, he'd been ready for it, but Lyss had been having a harder time wrapping her mind around the idea. Actually, she was having a harder time opening her heart to the idea. She was so afraid of setting herself up for a pain like they'd once had.

But seeing her like this, her eyes shining with excitement and joy. Yeah, she'd be alright. And she'd fall right back into motherhood.

It was a gift from their daughter. He just knew it. Her way of showing them they belonged together, and they were strong. It was her way of helping them find joy again in their lives.

Thank you, Katie.

"Come on. Let's get downstairs. Everyone's gonna start wondering what we're doing up here." He bobbed his eyebrows. "Of course, it's exactly what I am planning to do, it'll just have to wait until later."

Lyss laughed, a beautiful sound that happened all the time these days. "I'm gonna hold you to that."

As he turned to leave, she grabbed his arm. "Let's keep it to ourselves for now. It's so early." She shrugged.

Part of him was dying to shout it from the rooftops, but he got her point. It was too new. Hell, they hadn't even had a chance to process it themselves. No point in bringing everyone else in just yet. "Sure, babe. Come on." He captured her hand in his and tugged her out of the bathroom, giving her ass a swat when she passed him.

"Hey!" She yelped with a giggle.

"Can't help myself. That ass just calls to me."

They were still laughing when they reached the bottom of the steps. The staircase led directly into the kitchen, and all their friends were gathered around the kitchen island, loading plates and sharing stories. "Hold up a minute," he said as he snaked an arm around Alyssa's waist and pulled her back against him.

She tilted her head up and sent him a quizzical look.

"Just want to watch them all for a second. We've got it pretty damn good, don't we?"

Alyssa turned back and surveyed the jovial crowd. "Yeah, we really do."

"Ah, twenty bucks, Brett! Pay up." Alyssa's assistant Hannah held out her palm to Derek.

"What? No way, woman. How do you know you won? You can't possibly tell they weren't having sex up there."

Alyssa giggled at the same time Hannah rolled her eyes.

"Clothes are straight, hair isn't mussed, lipstick perfect. Please, *man*, no sex was being had. Pay up, sore loser."

Brett frowned and turned toward them. "Well?"

Derek laughed, long and loud. "Sorry to disappoint you, brother."

"Dude!" Brett said. He reached into his pocket, pulled out a bill, and slapped it in a grinning Hannah's palm.

She did a little dance before putting it into her pocket. "Pleasure doing business with you, sir," she said.

"Yeah, yeah." Brett grabbed a potato off Hannah's plate then hopped away before she could slap his arm.

Against his chest, Alyssa shook with laughter.

Suddenly, Derek couldn't hold it in. "Lyss is pregnant."

The room went dead silent except for his wife's loud gasp. She looked up at him. "What happened to keeping it quiet?"

He shrugged. "Sorry, slipped out." Hopefully his grin looked somewhat sheepish, though really, he wasn't remorseful in the least.

Lyss rolled her eyes and huffed. "Der, you were a SEAL. You were trusted with covert information all the time. You're supposed to be able to keep a secret for more than five seconds."

"Holy shit!" Roxie jumped up and down sending the mimosa in her champagne flute sloshing all over the floor. It was the first time in weeks she seemed to forget whatever was plaguing her and act just like Roxie. "Oh, shit, sorry! You're pregnant. Really? I'm gonna be an auntie?"

Lyss gave him a mock scowl then lifted up and kissed his chin before turning to her friend. "Yes," she squealed then bounded into the kitchen. Neither of them seemed to care much about the mess on the floor.

Derek leaned his shoulder against the wall at the foot of the staircase and watched as the most important people in his life made memories together. Not long ago, he'd worried they'd never get to the point where they felt life was good again. But they did. They'd suffered, and would never forget that period of their life, but as he'd hoped, they emerged from the darkness into a light that burned bright.

Nothing could or would break the bond he and Alyssa shared. It was strong as steel. The universe had thrown its very worst at them and they found the strength to survive. Sure, life wasn't perfect. They'd always have their fair share of complications. But in that moment, surrounded by the people they loved and who loved them, knowing a new life was growing inside Lyss…yeah, their life was pretty fucking sweet.

He was home.

Thank you so much for reading **Escapades**. If you enjoyed it, please consider leaving a review on Amazon or Goodreads.

Other books by Lilly Atlas

No Prisoners MC Sereis
Hook: A No Prisoners Novella
Striker
Jester
Acer
Lucky
Snake

Hell's Handlers MC Series
Zach
Maverick
Jigsaw
Copper

Join Lilly's mailing list for a **FREE** No Prisoners short story.
www.lillyatlas.com

Zach Preview

Tennessee 2008

It was finally fucking over.

Or maybe it was just beginning.

Either way, years, *years* of busting his ass, taking shit, and being treated like a worthless maggot were finished.

The vote was unanimous.

He was finally a brother.

Well, he was ninety-nine-point-nine percent of the way in. They couldn't just vote him in and chuck him the patch he'd been salivating over for the past three years. No, they had to throw in one last challenge, and a bitch of a test it was.

A branding. The Hell's Handlers Motorcycle Club emblem. On the left forearm. It was as important as the patches on the leather cut each brother wore. So important, if a man was tatted on his left forearm he couldn't even prospect. No, the emblem had to be seared into clean skin, so anyone and everyone would know who belonged to the motorcycle club.

And if being branded wasn't bad enough, there were rules that went along with the barbaric ceremony.

Every brother had to be in attendance. Heckling, ribbing, waiting to see just how much the new member wanted to be a part of the life. Waiting for them to crack.

No screaming.

No tears.

No passing out.

A grunt of pain was allowed, but beyond that, any outward show of weakness would null and void the unanimous vote to end the prospecting period and make him a fully-patched member of the Hell's Handlers MC.

He wouldn't make a peep. They could cut his fucking arm off and beat him with it and Zach still wouldn't utter a sound. That patch was his, and the only way he'd give it up was if some lucky motherfucker managed to pry it from his cold dead hands. Even then, he'd haunt the bastard and wear the thing as a spirit.

A shrill whistle cut through the raucous laughter and drunken male partying. Usually, the sound of fucking joined with the rest of the noise, but not tonight. This was just for the men, brothers in all but blood. At least this early part of the night. After Zach got his patch, they'd bring in the club pussy and he'd have his pick of the litter. One, two, hell even three women if he wanted. He'd earned it watching brother after brother partake in the sweet privilege that was not bestowed on prospects. Club pussy was for patched members only.

And now he was one.

His dick twitched in his pants but died the moment his president spoke. "Okay, fuckers, listen up."

All around him, his soon to be new brothers lowered their drinks and gave their president, Copper, their full attention. At twenty-nine, Copper was young to be in the role of club president, and since he'd been at it for almost four years already, he was officially the youngest leader in the club's near fifty-year history.

"We're just minutes away from welcoming another brother into the club. Shit, Zach's been one of the best prospects we've had. Tough as fuckin' nails, pulls more than his own weight, never runs his mouth, loyal." A puff of steam drifted from Copper's mouth as he spoke to the group.

The prez wasn't one to be fucked with. A good few inches over six feet, with a beard the color of a dirty penny, and plenty of hair to match, he was mean as a starving pit-bull. But Copper had the respect of every man in the club. Not just because he was the president, but because he'd earned it dragging the club from the brink of disaster and making it a thriving brotherhood once again.

Zach blew on his hands, trying to infuse some warmth into the frozen digits. The night air was colder than a witch's titty and standing around shirtless for the past half hour hadn't helped anything.

"Just one more test of this asshole's strength before we let him be one of us. Ready boys?" Copper waved Zach over to the mountain of wood crackling and spitting sparks. Sticking out of the bonfire, a long branding iron roasted away, just waiting to scorch some of Zach's skin.

Shouts of encouragement and a few hecklers betting on how much of a pussy he was and what octave his scream would hit, reached him as he made his way to the fire and his waiting president. Careful to keep his expression neutral he drew up next to his prez and waited. Wasn't that the whole point? Act like he wasn't scared. Wasn't about to shit his pants in anticipation of what would probably be the worse physical pain he'd ever experienced.

Fuckin' Copper's beard split and his teeth gleamed in the flickering fire. Prez lived for this bull. And if he didn't, he sure acted like he did with that shitty grin of anticipation. "Anything you want to say first?"

Zach shook his head while he bounced on the balls of his feet, hitting his pecs as hard as he could. Maybe if he could get some pain going somewhere else, the burn of the iron wouldn't be so bad.

"Won't work," Copper said as though reading his mind. "Tried the same thing when I was in your spot. Ain't nothing gonna make this shit any better." He bent and retrieved a bottle from next to his foot. Zach had no idea what it was full of, moonshine probably. "You know the drill. Bottle in your left hand. Ten seconds to drink as much as you can. Hold your arm out straight. I'll mark ya. No dropping the bottle. No spilling. No screaming. No puking. Stay on your feet for two whole minutes. Then you're a fuckin' brother."

Zach nodded. His chest rose and fell in a rapid rhythm as his breathing increased and the blood sped up in his veins. After blowing out a breath, he grabbed the bottle and brought it to his lips, tilting his head back and opening his throat as much as he could.

Some of the nastiest hooch he'd ever tasted filled his mouth and flowed down his throat, burning a path to his stomach. Ironic really, since he was about to be burned all to a crisp anyway. Somewhere, in the distance, he could hear his soon to be brothers cheering like a bunch of wild baboons, but he managed to drown out most of the noise. All but the sound of Copper counting down from ten.

"Three…two…one…arm!"

Zach tore the bottle from his lips and extended his arm. Unable to look away, he stared in fascinated horror as the glowing end of the iron made contact with the thin skin of his forearm. There was a fraction of a second where his eyes registered the flesh-to-iron connection, but the pain hadn't yet reached his brain.

And then it did.

All-consuming, searing pain like he'd never experienced fired through his nerve endings. Though the spot being branded was no bigger than a silver dollar, agony seemed to encompass his entire body until he couldn't recognize where it originated from. There was also an audible singe accompanied by the stench of melting flesh.

Blinding pain was a phrase he'd heard before, but now he'd lived it. Darkness clouded his vision and he slammed his knees back, determined not to give into the blissful oblivion that hovered just out of reach.

All around him, men screamed and hollered, but he couldn't make out their cries over the rushing in his ears. Nostrils flaring with each forceful inhalation and exhalation, he mashed his teeth together probably pulverizing the enamel as he fought to remain conscious.

Then the nausea hit. Instead of helping to lessen the pain, the damn moonshine sloshed in his gut and started a trip back up his esophagus, just as disgusting the second time around.

His eyes locked with Copper's. The grinning bastard was definitely enjoying it. All the more motivation to remain standing, quiet, and avoid vomiting the moonshine all over.

Copper pulled the iron away and tossed it to the ground, but it did nothing to diminish the agony. After what seemed like an eternity, he pulled his gaze away and checked his watch. Seconds ticked by slower than the thickest motor oil dripping from an engine. Finally, Copper looked at him again and this time his smile was genuine, welcoming. "Two minutes, brother."

Brother. Sweeter fucking words had never been spoken.

Copper grabbed him by the elbow and held up his throbbing arm. The pain was still there, but now the rush of excitement at achieving his three-year long goal overrode the worst of it. That and the moonshine was kicking in.

With a loud whoop of triumph, Copper held up Zach's branded arm. "Say hello to your newest brother, men." Cheers rose up all around.

Zach swayed on his feet as pain and nausea still warred for victory over his consciousness.

Copper whistled, reigning in the crazy. "He's now to be shown the respect any other brother receives. He's going to make a damn fine addition to the club."

Zach's chest constricted as pride surged.

"Proud of you, brother," Copper said, for Zach's ears only. "You were one hell of a prospect and you'll be one hell of an addition to the club."

"Thanks, Prez."

Raising his voice again, Copper turned to the rowdy crowd. "Now someone get Zach a beer and some pussy. The man's waited long enough."

They wouldn't be giving him any pain medication for the burn but losing his dick in a club girl should take care of the last of the discomfort.

Brothers converged on him from all angles, slapping his back and welcoming him. Not only would the moment be burned into his skin forever, but it was seared into his brain as well.

Best night of his life.

He was in.

Now it was time to set his sights on an executive position.

Enforcer would do quite nicely.

About the Author

Lilly Atlas is an award-winning contemporary romance author. She's a proud Navy wife and mother of three spunky girls. Every time Lilly downloads a new eBook she expects her Kindle App to tell her it's exhausted and overworked, and to beg for some rest. Thankfully that hasn't happened yet so she can often be found absorbed in a good book.

www.ingramcontent.com/pod-product-compliance
Lightning Source LLC
Chambersburg PA
CBHW060935180626
46817CB00004B/1559